Praise for Barbara Jean Coast's
Poppy Cove Mystery Series

"I thoroughly enjoyed reading *Strangled by Silk*—a
very good read, and a very fun read. I grant it my Five-
Kitty seal of approval."

—*Jane Reads*

"Barbara Jean Coast's debut novel *Strangled by Silk* (A
Poppy Cove Mystery) is a hit! Pick up this book today
for a trip back in time to the 50's! You will love it!"

—*Shelley's Book Case*

"I loved this book. It is fashionable (because I love the
fashions at Poppy Cove), charming, witty, mysterious,
with interesting characters, a little romance and all the
things I love about a cozy mystery."

—Julie Seedorf, author of the
Fuchsia, Minnesota
mystery series

Death of a Beauty Queen

(A Poppy Cove Mystery)

by

Barbara Jean Coast

Janice,
Welcome back
to Poppy Cove!
Toodles,
Barbara Jean Coast
aka
Andrea & Heather

For information, email **Cozy Cat Press**, cozycatpress@aol.com or visit our website at: www.cozycatpress.com

COZY CAT
P R E S S

ISBN: 978-1-939816-43-6
Printed in the United States of America

Cover design by Nicole Spence
http:www.covershotcreations.com

1 2 3 4 5 6 7 8 9 10

Author's Note and Acknowledgements

The Poppy Cove Mysteries are a work of fiction, loosely based on the Santa Barbara region in the late 50's/early 60's. Our civic royalties and social events of both our fictional and factual towns fall under creative license. We think it would have been really fun to be known as the Dairy Queen—in reality, we sometimes feel like a couple of Dilly Bars!

So many people have been so loving and supportive with us while we've been telling our tales—our friends and families, our newfound writer friends and Poppy Cove Fans—we thank you so much. Michael Redmond, the Director of Research at the Santa Barbara Historical Museum has been there from day one, answering any of our questions in lightning speed, regardless of how trivial or benign they may have been. KKJZ has provided a swinging background to our writing days, giving a little swizzle into Barbara Jean's heels. It's all been greatly appreciated. We feel very blessed and grateful to be taken in by Patricia Rockwell at Cozy Cat Press, and so enjoy the camaraderie of our fellow Cozy Catters—such a talented and warm group that keeps on inspiring and encouraging us.

Warm Regards to All,
Andrea Taylor and Heather Shkuratoff
aka Barbara Jean Coast

You are cordially invited to the

Tenth Annual Santa Lucia
Hospital Charity Ball

Santa Lucia Yacht Club
100 Oceanview Drive
Santa Lucia, California

Saturday, September 28,
1957.
Cocktail Reception 5:30 pm.

CHAPTER ONE

"And now ladies, in our final ensemble, Miss Santa Lucia!" exclaimed Dirk Roberts, the suave and dapper local radio announcer. Nora Burbank swished and sashayed her way through the crowd in a fiery red silk satin that was lovely against her tanned, toned skin. The dress had a strapless fitted bodice finished at the top with a two-inch fold that sloped to "v" in the back and a column sheath skirt that fell to the ankle. At the waist was a rhinestone rectangular belt clasp for the detachable train that shimmered and pooled behind the beautiful young girl.

Margot Williams, designer of the dress, watched nervously from the side curtain off the stage into the dimmed room. Easing into a proud smile, she watched Nora carry it off perfectly with a womanly, yet girlish charm. All eyes were on Nora as the ballroom orchestra played their rendition of "Diamonds are a Girl's Best Friend."

The dress had been a major feat of engineering with a built-in brassiere that was so firmly constructed that the gown could stand on its own. There had been a lot of last minute work and fittings to get it just right. It completely consumed Margot's attention over the past week at Poppy Cove, the two and a half year old design atelier and dress shop that she shared with her friend, Daphne Hunting-Smythe. It was located on the corner of Poppy Lane and Cove Street, which was the heart of downtown Santa Lucia, California.

Dirk took a sip from his water glass and described the dress to the crowd in the details Margot had provided for him. He continued his commentary. "And framing her lovely face is an exclusive diamond necklace, designed and created by our very own Isaac Mendelson of Mendelson's Quality Jewelers on Cove Street. Mendelson's Quality Jewelers—where your diamond dreams come true!"

The piece was stunning. Surrounding Nora's graceful, long neck and playing off of her short cut, jet-black hair and deep green eyes, was an elaborate web of small diamonds with larger stones worked into the design in an artfully created pattern that sparkled, casting off subtle prisms in the twilight setting of the room.

Daphne, who was the accessories buyer as well as partner in Poppy Cove, was standing beside Margot, peeking around the edge of the stage curtain. She had organized all the purses, shoes and the rest of the accessories for the show. She was pleased to see that the quality paste offerings they sold in the store and featured in the event were able to shine proud next to the real thing. They'd made the right decision to use exclusive and impressive gems in the grand finale.

Even Baroness Eva von Eissen, who was herself dripping in diamonds from head to toe, was impressed with the Mendelson piece. A recent immigrant of vague European royal descent, the baroness had made her presence known in Santa Lucia society. Although she had only arrived in the past month, she'd made an enormous donation to the hospital fund that assured her invitation to the sold out gala event. She showed up dressed in an old-fashioned black lace gown, which appeared to be a family heirloom garment from the Victorian age. It was very out of place compared to the voluminous ball gowns in silky shimmering hues that were the happy glamour of the times. She eyed the necklace with a greedy glint in her eye.

She wasn't the only one. As Nora walked around the tables, audible *oohs* and *aahs* could be heard from the crowd, which was mainly made up of Mendelson's and Poppy Cove's clientele. Elaine Stinson, the pleasant and discreet mayor's wife, leaned over to her companions at her table, smiling and murmuring approval. Nancy Lewis, the social climbing wife of the manager of the First Bank of Santa Lucia, snapped at her daughter Barbara, telling her to pay attention and sit up straight, in the meantime preening towards the flashing camera of Jake Moore, a *Santa Lucia Times* photographer who'd positioned himself near their table under the guidance of Loretta Simpson, the paper's Society Editor.

The rest of the young ladies, six in total, including the first and second Miss Santa Lucia Princesses, were dressed in the Holiday Soirée designs as well. They followed Nora at a discreet distance around the floor and joined her on the stage. Daphne and Margot snuck out the side door, briskly walking to the back of the room to watch the finale. The models in their shimmering skirts of jewel-toned moiré and velvet paired with white charmeuse blouses, full evening gowns in brocade and solid hues, and cocktail length dresses complimented the collection. The girls gracefully floated down the side stairs and curled their way through the crowd, re-joining Nora at the end back onstage. As the orchestra finished their song, Jake and Loretta placed themselves down low in front of the stage, snapping away and scribbling notes respectively.

Daphne and Margot stifled giddy giggles as they realized they had pulled off a nearly perfect show. There had been the usual mishaps—a quick fix to a hem, a tuck here, smeared lipstick retouched there, a spritz of hair spray at the last minute, but the timing had been a dream. Nora had only a small misstep with her first princess that no one saw and there had been no falls in public. The girls moved quickly and silently back to their post behind the stage.

Sarah Browning, the recently appointed chairwoman of the Santa Lucia Hospital Charity Ball, glowed at the head table, dabbing her eyes. She was so happy she was moved to tears at the success of the evening but also sad that her dear friend and planner of the event, Constance Stearns-Montgomery, would never be there again. Her murder, just over a month ago, still greatly affected the entire town. Sarah considered how she would address the matter in her closing speech at the end of the show. She stood up and made her way to the platform and positioned herself between Nora and her attendants.

"I would like to thank our beautiful young ladies for giving us such a lovely treat and for the always entertaining commentary from our very own Dirk Roberts." There was a round of applause from the audience as Sarah gestured at the models and nodded at the announcer's podium. He raised his glass in her direction and took another swig. "Constance Stearns-Montgomery always worked tirelessly year round to support the Santa Lucia Hospital Charity Ball and as you are all aware, is no longer with us," her voice started to quiver. "She would have been so proud. Let's all take a moment of silence to remember the efforts of our dear friend."

For the most part, the room became deathly silent, except for the audible squirming and huffing coming from the direction of the Lewis table. Nancy Lewis and Constance Stearns-Montgomery had not been the best of friends and often had disagreements in public, always incited by Mrs. Lewis.

The moment gave Sarah a chance to compose herself and carry on. "I would like to personally show my gratitude to Patricia Huntington-Smythe for stepping in at the last minute to help organize tonight's event and to take the opportunity to announce her newly elected position of assistant chair on the Santa Lucia Hospital Charity Committee." There was a polite round of applause, punctuated with a *harrumph* of disapproval once again from Nancy. She felt she had been overlooked for the vacancy, even though she rarely attended the meetings and tended to vote against the majority, no matter what the issue was. "And finally, please join me in toasting the two women who made this fashion show happen—Margot Williams and Daphne Huntington-Smythe of Poppy Cove." The audience rose to their feet and gave the girls a standing ovation as they made their way onto the stage and stood next to Nora and Sarah.

Dirk directed the dining room wait staff to present the shop owners, the chairwoman and models with bouquets of roses. As Nora was being presented with her flowers, Mary Ann Rutherford, First Princess, stepped forward to accept the bouquet. The young waiter made worried eye contact with Nora, as he was instructed to give the flowers to her. Gracefully, Nora gently moved forward, outstretching her hands to receive the roses and an embarrassed Mary Ann took a step backwards, looked around and believing no one saw her faux pas during the crowd's applause, returned to her place in line.

As the noise wound down, Daphne spoke first. "Thank you all for attending. We hope you enjoyed the show." The girls were happy to hear a murmur of approval throughout the room. "We would also like to thank Hank and Laura Wright from Wright's Shoes for providing the beautiful patent and satin pumps worn this evening, and a very special thank you to Mendelson's Quality Jewelers for their very first participation in our annual event."

Daphne smiled and nodded to Margot who continued. "We would also like to thank Mr. Anthony and his assistant, Todd, for tonight's hair and make-up, as well as Gloria from Poppy Lane Florists for the flower arrangements. And, of course, to our staff at Poppy Cove, who worked so hard. We could not have done this without them."

As the applause died down again, Dirk spoke from his emcee post. "Yes, ladies, and don't forget that everything you saw in this evening's show is available for purchase. Visit Wright's Shoes, Mendelson's Quality Jewelers, Poppy Lane Florists and, of course, Poppy Cove to place your orders. Now on with our evening. Why not take the time for a walk out in the gardens or along the harbor while the room gets set up for the dance? It's a beautiful night!" A gentle, warm breeze wafted in as the attendants opened up the French doors onto the garden off of the Tropical Ballroom. In the distance, the sun was barely visible above the ocean in the fogless glowing twilight.

The crowd on the stage made their way to the back while the musicians took a break and tuned up for the rest of the night's entertainment. The ladies in the audience took the opportunity to stroll in the fresh air and join their husbands who had now emerged from the Palms Dining Room where they had remained during the fashion show, talking business, drinking brandy and smoking cigars.

Daphne and Margot were elated with how things had gone. They joined Marjorie, their head seamstress; Irene, their store manager; and Betty and Abigail, their shop staff in a joyful group embrace, laughing and talking loudly about their success and commenting on some of their avoided catastrophes—the mix-up with the dresses hemmed for two different girls switched, one a tall size four, the other a rather petite size twelve. Both were at opposite ends of the room, which caused a blind panic before they all realized what had happened. The earring that snagged on a wrap and took forever to untangle and the poor girl who got hair spray in her eye as she turned her head to look at another one's dress. Everyone realized for the most part that it went smoothly.

Nora ran up to Margot and gave her a huge hug. "Miss Williams! Thank you so much for my dress! It's so beautiful!" The showpiece gown now belonged to her in her capacity as Miss Santa Lucia. Every year, the pageant committee commissioned Poppy Cove to create an ensemble for Miss Santa Lucia's reigning queen to wear to the rest of her formal functions throughout her term. The pageant was held in May, coinciding with Santa Lucia Founders' Days. As part of the competition, Poppy Cove held a summer fashion show featuring the contestants. At that time, the winning queen and her attendants also received formal dresses created at the shop, courtesy of the town. The ladies were to wear them to all the events they attended on behalf of Santa Lucia. "Do I get to keep the necklace, too?" Nora asked with flushed excitement.

Margot laughed at the question and stroked her arm. "No, it has to go back to Mendelson's. We should remove it now, it's incredibly expensive."

"That would be a fine idea." Efrem Goldberg confirmed as he came in from the back stage door with his wife, Rebecca. Betty's husband Dwight was in tow along with Eddie, Irene's date following in behind them. "Isaac's been very secretive about the piece. He doesn't know that I put it in the show, but I think it was a smart move. He'll be singing a different tune once he sees the business it brings in." Efrem was Isaac's son-in-law, married to his only child, Rebecca. He was apprenticing at Mendelson's to take over when Isaac deemed fit to retire. "I better get it back in the store safe tonight before he knows it's not there."

As Margot moved to Nora's nape to remove the showpiece, Eddie swooped in front of the girl and began fingering the necklace. He gave a low wolf whistle. With his hair slicked back into a D.A., greaser jeans, white T-shirt and beat up black leather bomber jacket, he looked like he belonged at a rumble, rather than a posh country club. "Hey buddy, how much do one of these set ya back?"

Nora's eyes grew wide as she was startled by Eddie's approach and backed into Margot. "Cool it, girly. I ain't meanin' ya no harm. I'm just thinkin' how these rocks would look on my babe. Whadda ya say, Reney? Treat me right and maybe it's yours," he smirked.

Irene gave him a look that would chill Siberia. "Just stay out of the way, Eddie." She gestured to the back wall where Dirk had parked himself, nursing his glass. "Go wait for me over there." Dirk saluted his glass and waved him over. Eddie gave a grimace, grabbed a bottle from the refreshment table and took his place in the shadows.

Eddie clinked his bottle to Dirk's glass as the pair held up the wall. "Ladies love the diamonds," Dirk passed on his slurring pearls of wisdom to his new companion. "Don't listen to her. If you did give her that, she'd be eating out of your hand."

"Ya think so?"

Dirk nodded. "Yep. I'm thinking myself that a piece like that would win my wife, or ex-wife, as she calls it, back."

"Is she worth that kind of dough?"

"Ask her lawyer." Dirk took another swig and helped himself to a refill from Eddie's bottle. "She sure was a looker. 'Bout twenty years ago, she was wearing that sash." Kathy Newman Roberts, Dirk's ex-wife 'Kitty,' had been Miss Santa Lucia in her time. After fifteen years of a childless marriage, so they wouldn't ruin her figure, she took off with a younger man to Bel Air, telling Dirk she was tired of a man with no future and found one who was going places, currently on Dirk's alimony payments. "A one time purchase like that would cost less than what I'm paying now."

Eddie squinted in his direction, eying him up and down. "You got that kind of change just lyin' around?"

"Nah, but if I could get it, it'd be worth it."

Eddie shrugged. "I dunno. I mean Irene's a good time, but there's other live wires out there. Spendin' too much money on a dame may give her the wrong idea. Like I'm serious or somethin'. Might just be buyin' a lifetime of trouble."

Dirk sighed. "Yeah, but what a trouble that lifetime can be." He gave a sly, surly grin in the direction of the women.

Efrem walked over to Nora and Margot with a couple of black velvet cases in hand. Daphne was on his left and he handed her one of the cases as he opened the remaining one. Margot removed the necklace from Nora's neck by the back clasp and carefully handed it to Efrem. He placed it with great care on the satin mold and closed the lid. He switched the boxes with Daphne and opened up the new one. He slipped a beautifully crafted paste replica on the girl. "Here, you can keep this one." He smiled as he handed Nora the empty case. "Use this to protect it when you're not wearing it. It may not be the real gems, but it's pretty special, too. I took great care with the settings. It should last you a lifetime."

"Thanks." Nora was polite, but a little disappointed. The necklace, although exact in setting, had a slightly lower sheen than the one she'd been wearing. Always poised, she recovered quickly. "It looks great with the dress, too!"

"What do I get to keep? Do I get one, too?" Mary Ann Rutherford swept her way over from the dressing area.

Margot eyed her coolly and then looked over her shoulder at Caroline Parker, the second Miss Santa Lucia Princess. "As Nora's court attendants, you and Caroline do get to keep your dresses and pearl chokers." Their dresses were similar to Nora's in that they were strapless, but in a shimmery icy blue satin with a higher back. They did not have a train but did have the same rhinestone belt clasp. In their simpler cut, they complemented the queen's fiery red attire.

"Oh," Mary Ann pouted. "That's too bad. With my longer nape I think Nora's necklace would be much more suitable on me. See?" She grabbed the box from Daphne's hands, scooped the necklace out and placed it around the front of her throat.

The crowd was startled. Efrem stepped forward and took the necklace and box from the girl. "I'll take that." He gingerly inspected the necklace and put it carefully back in its place.

Mary Ann moved closer in on Efrem, stroking the box slowly, seductively. "Now, don't you think that my body would be a better canvas for your art?"

Efrem harrumphed and blushed, protectively pulling the jewel case out of her reach and glancing at Rebecca for support, who was raising her eyebrows at the galling young girl.

Nora walked over to Mary Ann and firmly grabbed her arm, taking her aside. "Why are you behaving like this? First you almost trip me on the way out to the floor, then you try to steal my flowers, and now this. What has gotten into you?"

Mary Ann's frosty blue eyes met Nora's. "I, I don't know," she stammered. "It just seems like you get it all, and I get nothing. Not even fake diamonds."

Nora softened a little and replied. "That's not true. You get your dress, the choker, the title of First Princess and still get to go almost everywhere I do." Mary Ann shrugged and sniffled. "Now pull yourself together. We have a position to keep!"

"There you are! They're expecting you out in the ballroom. The first dance is about to start," Tina Burbank, a slightly older-looking version of her daughter, came back stage to retrieve Nora. "You're supposed to dance with your escort in the first number." She stepped back to look at her daughter and Mary Ann. "Is everything all right?" Nora's parents, the dentist Dr. Edward Burbank and Tina were prominent members of Santa Lucia society. Tina was also a member of the hospital charity committee. If she got wind that there was a problem, she could alert the pageant authorities and there could be trouble. The girls looked at each other, Nora wary, Mary Ann contrite, but silently called a truce and both nodded at Mrs. Burbank, avoiding a scene. Mary Ann left quietly without a fuss while the attention was no longer on her. Satisfied with their answers, Tina turned to address Margot and Daphne. "Ladies, the show was great! Now Nora, come along, we've got to go!" She was always good-natured, but always in a hurry.

"Oh no, you don't, you're a mess!" Mr. Anthony came rushing over, brush in one hand, hair spray in the other. "What will people think if I let you out in public looking like this?" Others in the back stage area all looked at each other, smirking. Other than one or two locks of hair relaxing on the back of Nora's nape, she looked polished and beautiful. The diminutive blonde man continued to fuss. "Todd? Todd! Where are you? We need that lipstick, now."

"Right here, no need to make a scene." Lanky Todd strode over. As Mr. Anthony's assistant and cosmetician at his salon, he was used to his employer's over the top blustering. He gave a critical look at Nora's face and with one quick swipe of Crimson Dream cream lipstick he pronounced her ready for the ball. "There. She's beautiful again." Todd gave her a smile and a reassuring pat on the shoulder.

Mr. Anthony walked around Nora as she smiled expectantly at him. "Yes, absolutely charming. My dear, you are the perfect queen!"

"Not the only one," came a muttered slur from a corner. Dirk Roberts' demeanor changed as he continued to sip at his water glass, refilling it from the vodka bottle among the other backstage refreshments. "Ah, let her go. The girls are all beautiful, every last one of them." He weaved up from his slouching position against the wall and wobbled as he waved his glass in the air. "Everyone, join me in a toast—to all the beautiful women in this room. Ladies!" He took another big gulp and thumped back against the wall. His newfound partner in crime, Eddie, snorted and laughed beside him.

Tina Burbank gave a nervous twitter. "Yes, well, we must be going. Can't keep the orchestra waiting," and ushered her girl back out to the ballroom. Nora was the only girl in the fashion show who was attending the dance.

"Yesss, time is money. Can't keep people waitin'. How 'bout you, honey? Waitin' for me?" Dirk had slid a little further along the wall and leaned up to the sly and beautiful Irene.

"Oh, lay off. I've had your kind for breakfast," she uttered as she gave him a shove in the other direction, knocking him into Eddie who yelped when his bottle splashed up on him. Irene was nobody's fool. "And Eddie, that's it. Find your own way home. I've got bigger plans than you." She'd seen her share of oafs and a drunken local emcee and a small town thug were nothing she couldn't handle. Irene turned on her patent black stiletto heels, her cherry red full skirt swishing in her wake, and faced her employers. "Do you still need me tonight?"

It was obvious to Margot that Irene wanted to leave, but they still had a lot to pack up. Marjorie stepped in, remarking, "Honestly Irene, take a look around you. There's still so much that we need to do before calling it a night." Irene fell back into line and quietly got involved in the tasks at hand.

"We should be on our way, too. I'd like to get this back into Isaac's safe. What'd you say we meet up at the diner across from Martin's on Cove Street?" Efrem turned to Dwight. "We'll be about half an hour. Will you be done here by then, Betty?"

Betty looked at her employers. Margot and Daphne nodded as they were organizing the wares to go back to the shop. "Yes, I think that'll be fine. Whoever gets to Charlie's first gets the table!" The couples had planned to go out for the evening after the show. Rebecca and Betty had been friends in high school and it was the first time since Rebecca had moved back from Los Angeles with her husband that they would go on a double date. As the Goldbergs left, Betty realized she had to give her husband Dwight something to do, as he was looking lost and out of place. Although they would be going out for burgers and fries, Dwight could always eat. It kept him busy and he did have a bottomless pit for a stomach. She fixed him a plate of cold cuts and salads along with a drink and situated him in a folding chair near the refreshment table to keep him occupied while she helped her employers finish up for the evening. Dwight, a young salesman at Smart's Oldsmobiles who was more used to a roomful of cars and professional men, sat uncomfortably with all the fashion show fuss and the rogue's gallery in the corner. He grabbed Betty's arm, gently but firmly, with pleading eyes. "You won't be long, will you?" in a tone more desperate than angry. She patted his arm and smiled to herself as she went to work.

"Thank you so much for the dress. It's lovely!" Second princess Caroline Parker gave a little twirl. The gown emphasized her shapely bare shoulders that had a pretty little sprinkle of freckles, making her look golden with her shimmering auburn pageboy. "I think I'll just wear it home. My mom is picking me up any moment. She'll love it!" She gave Margot a quick squeeze and left by the side door.

The Poppy Cove staff got busy helping the rest of the models change out of the show dresses behind the changing screens at the far side of the room. Other than the gowns belonging to the Miss Santa Lucia royalty, all of the other garments worn by the other girls had to go back to the shop in pristine condition. Abigail, Betty, Irene and Marjorie passed the garments to Margot who hung them on the racks with great care and tucked them into the huge plastic coverings while Daphne laid out the necklaces, earrings and other accessories in large rectangular boxes for safekeeping. They packed up the shoes for Wright's in their original boxes with the stays and tissue paper. Everything would stay there until Monday morning, when a local delivery truck would pick up the goods and take them back to Poppy Cove.

After Daphne was satisfied that all the accessories had been neatly tucked away, she whisked behind dressing screens to change into her own ball gown. The Poppy Cove owners had been beautifully attired in their day dresses suitable for that evening's tasks, but Daphne was staying to attend the dance. Her family, the Huntington-Smythes, were long standing members of the Santa Lucia community and attended every year, as well as the other important social club events. She hung up her turquoise cotton lawn shirtdress on a rack to pick up later and slipped into a shimmering gown of pale celadon silk that floated with a tulle overskirt, setting off her sun-kissed skin and short, wavy blond hair.

Margot was straightening the racks when she felt a pair of strong arms circle her waist. "Excuse me, but I think it's time for a dance." She smiled and turned around, seeing Santa Lucia Police Detective Tom Malone, attired in his formal dress uniform for the event. He was the epitome of tall, dark and handsome, taking Margot's breath away. They had been an item for a couple of years; both very busy in their careers and happy in their relationship, while others wondered when the wedding bells would ring.

She gave him a quick peck on the lips. "Oh, I've got too much to do. Besides, I'm not dressed for the ball!" Margot had no intention of going out on the dance floor. She was pleased to see Tom, especially when he looked so handsome tonight, and was hoping to go out for a nightcap with him and then off to dreamland, not dancing the night away.

"Nonsense! We've got plenty of dresses here for you to choose from. Stay and join Dan and me! It'll be a blast!" Daphne effused as she came out from behind the screen, giving her skirt a primp. She looked up and saw her fair-haired Daniel Henshaw, who had come in with Tom. He was her latest beau and when she saw his tall sporty frame all decked out in black tie her eyes lit up even brighter, but she winced when she looked down at herself. The strapless, fitted bodice featured her shapely arms, toned from her athletic lifestyle of tennis, golf and swimming at the club, as well as her newfound interest in surfing whenever she could find the time. However, there were still the remnants of nasty bruises on her arms from when she'd been in a struggle a couple of weeks ago. There was no longer any pain, other than a little hurt pride when she realized she had stumbled into a murderous trap. "Todd, could you do something about this? Do you have a matching foundation of cover-up cream?"

"Wow. Who'd a thought you'd like it rough?" sniggered Eddie, elbowing his newfound friend in the corner. Dan shot Tom a look and the two went over to Eddie and Dirk who were barely holding up the wall.

"Good evening, gentlemen. How are we doing tonight?" Tom went into full police mode.

Dirk did his best to straighten up. "Ossifer, we're jus' fine."

Tom watched the man slide over to his cohort. "What kind of trouble are you getting up to now, Eddie?"

"Aw, nuthin'. I'm just waitin' on my girl. That one there, the dishy one, aren't ya, honey?" he indicated with his glass.

"Not anymore," Irene muttered. "Policeman Tom, I want nothing to do with him."

Tom sized up the situation. "Dan, can you go find Riley while I keep an eye on these two? They'll need a lift home tonight."

Dirk nodded and took another sip. Eddie commented, "Jus' drop me off at the track. I got people to meet."

"Nothing doing. Your night is over. You'll be escorted home or bunking up in the tank tonight, your choice." Tom stood firm, as he looked him straight on while Eddie whined and weaved. He tried to stare him down to no avail and muttered a street address as Officer Riley showed up to take care of the men.

"So what do you think, Todd? Can you make this go away for the night?" Daphne brought the conversation back to her bruises. Dwight still sat quietly, watching all the action, waiting for Betty and nibbling on his cold cuts.

"I think so." Todd brought over his make-up palette, which was housed in a red metal tool kit and started to gently touch up her arm. "There. That looks pretty good. It's oil-based so it should last all night. It'll set in about a minute, so just be careful not to get it on your dress till then." The foundation took away the discoloration and her arm looked perfect.

"Thanks!" She turned to Margot. "Well, what do you say? Have you picked out your gown?"

Margot hesitated. She loved the fashion show, but really didn't go in for formal balls and events. There was a side of her that was much more reserved and preferred to be working behind the scenes. "There's still so much more to do."

"Now, now then, Miss Margot. Betty, Irene and I can finish up. There's just a little more to do," Marjorie gently shooed and chided her employer. "Your young man wants to dance with you!"

Tom smiled and looked her in the eyes. "Yes, I do. Come on, just one quick dance and we'll go for a drink." He kissed her playfully on the lips and embraced her.

She laughed and said, "Oh, alright. It would be fun. Yes, let's!" Margot decided to stay in her lavender day dress, which looked quite fetching on her curvy frame with its slim bodice and wide skirt. The tone illuminated her fair complexion and auburn pageboy hair. The foursome went out to the ball, while Marjorie and her team finished up, shut off the lights and left for the night.

CHAPTER TWO

Marjorie was the first to arrive at eight thirty at Poppy Cove on Monday morning. She picked up the *Santa Lucia Times* newspaper from the front doorstep and placed it on the sales desk. She spread out the Society section front page that featured a lovely picture of Nora in her pageant dress and necklace, flanked on either side by the shop owners who were all smiles, looking young and beautiful. The head seamstress felt a sense of pride. She was the girls' first employee when they started their endeavor in the spring of 1955. She had a wealth of experience from working for many years as the head dressmaker at Martin's Department Store and had attired many of the town's ladies since they were young girls, including Daphne and her family. A widow in her mid-50's, she still had plenty of stamina, tempered with solid know-how to be interested in the challenge of the new store when the girls approached her with their novel business idea.

She went through to the back door of the workroom behind the sales floor to supervise the delivery of the goods from the yacht club. When the men were done unloading, she began looking over the racks of clothes, inspecting for any necessary repairs or cleaning.

Margot came in carrying a carafe of coffee and a box of muffins from the tearoom across the street. She glanced briefly at the article and smiled. She set down the morning goodies on the table in the lunchroom and joined Marjorie in the inspection. "Good morning. How do things look?"

"All things considered, quite well. So far I've only come across one or two fallen hems, and a loose button or two, but no stains or damage to be concerned about." She stopped and looked over the top frame of her glasses. "Did you and your Tom have a good evening? Did you stay long at the dance after all?" The older lady had a twinkle in her eye as she asked Margot about her love life. She liked Tom and was lately hinting to Margot that she should be lining him up for matrimony by now.

Marjorie was well meaning and good-natured, but sometimes took on too much of a mothering role as far as Margot was concerned. Marriage was a long way off in her mind, but she did think that she was beginning to truly love Tom. Right now, however, orders for the holiday season and a new spring collection were uppermost in her thoughts for her future. By all accounts, the fashion show had been a success. Even at the ball, the ladies were commenting to Daphne and Margot how much they admired the new collection, and a few of their regular customers had placed orders with them on the dance floor.

"We stayed for a couple of numbers. I actually enjoyed it. Daphne and Daniel looked like they were going to dance the night away." Marjorie's support staff, consisting of a patternmaker, cutter, presser and two seamstresses arrived for their shift. The shop was closed on Mondays, but the phone was always answered and the sewing room was in full swing. The telephone began to ring and Margot took another order from the show on the production room extension.

Although Monday was usually her day off, Irene arrived shortly for an extra shift and helped herself to a coffee. She clipped out the article and photo from the *Times* and filed them away for safekeeping. Margot brought out a carton of accessories to the front counter for Irene to sort through while she answered the phone for new appointments.

Daphne floated in about ten minutes later with a dreamy expression on her face. Irene rolled her eyes and muttered a cynical comment to herself. Daphne breezed past her, not noticing her grumbling, dropped into the lunchroom, grabbed a muffin and poured herself coffee. She continued on her way to the backroom and sat down at a worktable, absent-mindedly playing with a box of purses and belts from the delivery. "Hi," she sighed happily to her co-workers.

Margot and Marjorie smirked at each other. Margot asked her partner, "Back from the dance yet?"

"What? Oh yes, it was fine! I didn't know Daniel could dance like that. Did you know that he was voted 'Best Dancer' in his senior year at high school?"

Margot continued to go through the racks. "No, I didn't know that."

"He really is dreamy." Daphne had been seeing Daniel now for about a month. He was the riding instructor at the new Stearns Academy for Girls and full of surprises. He came from a wealthy background but chose to work hard with his hands to earn his keep and was equally at ease with a sunset ride in the hills as well as at formal society events. Daniel's mix of interests and abilities continued to entertain and intrigue Daphne, even if she did consider him as a possible murder suspect early on in their relationship. Albeit, an attractive, virile one. "We just kept dancing and dancing. We were the last ones left, I think. The sun was coming up by the time Dan took me home."

Margot let her friend continue. Daphne fell in love about four times a year. Fortunately when the new flame sizzled out, she didn't mope too long before the next man flickered onto the scene.

Daphne continued nattering about Daniel's amazing attributes and hidden talents as they were re-hanging the fashion show garments back on the sales floor racks. Lost in their own reveries, the girls were startled by a rattle of the door handle. Margot walked over to the entrance and saw a familiar face.

"Hello, Efrem." She unlocked the door and he came in urgently. "Is everything okay?"

He saw Irene sorting through the jewelry on the sales desk and rushed over to her. He was in such a panic that he almost knocked her down. She gave him a snarly look, but in his rush he didn't pay any attention to her. "Are these from the show?"

"Yes. Are you looking for something?" Irene stepped back and let him rifle through the pieces frantically. Margot and Daphne stopped what they were doing and came over to the sales counter.

"Is there more? Is that it?"

"There's another couple of boxes in the back," Daphne replied.

"Can you get them?"

"Sure. I'll be right back. What are you looking for?" Efrem didn't answer, just kept running the earrings, necklaces and bracelets through his hands. Daphne and Margot exchanged looks and went back to get the remaining boxes.

All the while, Margot tried to get Efrem to tell them what he was searching for. She eventually put her hands on his, stopped them from frantically sifting and asked, "Why don't you tell us what you need to find? Maybe we can help you."

"Paste. These are all just paste," Efrem muttered.

Daphne was mildly indignant as she nodded her head. "Of course they are. They may not be the real gems like you sell, but they're pretty nice pieces."

He held a strand in his hand. "No, no, the necklace. It's not real."

Daphne gently removed it from his hand. "That's right. It's a costume piece."

"No, not this one. The one at the store. It's not real."

"What store? Mendelson's?" As Daphne said it, the pieces were coming together. The shock began to register in her mind. Her eyes widened. "You mean the one in the velvet box from the show? Nora's?"

"Yes." Efrem huffed and ran a hand through his thick black hair. "They must have gotten switched. I took the necklace out of the safe this morning to check it over. I wanted to make sure there weren't any loose settings and I couldn't believe it. It's the replica."

"Are you sure?" Margot asked.

"Of course, I'm sure," he snapped. "Sorry, it's just, well…I was looking at it closely. It looks good, really good, but when I played around with it, I realized it had to be the one I made, not Isaac's original. I have to get it back before he figures it out. He hadn't come in yet this morning. Is it here?"

"No. I mean, I don't think so. Nora would have it. She was given the copy, remember?" Daphne paused. "Well, now what we thought was the copy, anyhow." Daphne smiled and gave him a reassuring pat on the arm. "I'll just call the Burbanks and explain the mix-up and ask them to bring the necklace to your shop."

"No, not there! Like I've said, Isaac doesn't know about it yet or at least I don't think he does. I left it tucked in the back of the safe. I'll keep him busy with other things," Efrem sighed and once again ran a hand over his head. "Have her bring it here and I'll come by and bring the replica. Do you think we could take care of this by this afternoon?"

"I'll call the Burbanks right away." Irene passed Daphne the address book on the desk, all the while keeping an eye on Efrem's erratic behavior. Daphne thumbed through the book and reached for the phone. She dialed the number, drumming her hand on the desk as Efrem paced back and forth. Her call was answered on the third ring.

"Burbank residence." There was a cool, calm female voice on the other end.

"Yes, hello. This is Daphne Huntington-Smythe of Poppy Cove. I would like to speak with Nora, please."

"I'm sorry, she's not in right now. I believe she's at school."

"Oh, is this Mrs. Burbank?" Daphne asked the woman as she twirled the phone cord in her hand, picking up on Efrem's nervousness while he waited.

"No, ma'am. This is Mae, the housekeeper. Mrs. Burbank isn't in either."

"Do you know when Nora will be home?"

"Well, dinnertime, I suppose. Would you like her to return your call?"

Daphne thought for a moment. That might be later than they would like. Efrem was practically jumping out of his skin. They'd be lucky if Irene didn't cold cock him, as she was giving him one of her impatient looks. "What about Mrs. Burbank? Will she be home earlier?"

"I expect so. She's lunching with the arts committee today and should be home around 2:30."

"Good. Could you have her call me right away when she gets in? It's very important that I reach her as soon as possible."

Mae took down the particulars. Daphne hung up the phone, faced Efrem and did her best to reassure him. "As soon as I hear from the Burbanks, I'll arrange for them to bring the necklace and let you know when they'll be here. Don't worry, we'll get this all resolved by the end of the day."

Efrem, resigned to the fact that he'd have to wait a little longer, sighed and slouched as he relaxed. " Okay, well, I guess I'll just go back to the shop and keep Isaac busy when he shows up with other things so he doesn't look too closely at the necklace in the safe. Once we know they're bringing the real piece in, I'll bring the replica over. Hopefully, it'll all go off without a hitch and my father-in-law will be none the wiser. I'll have enough to answer for once he finds out that I used it in the show. I've gotten rid of the store copy of the *Times* and he doesn't get the paper at his home, so he may not know what I've done yet. Once we get it all right and he sees how much business being in the fashion show brings in, he'll be okay, but I have to fix this first."

The girls felt a sense of relief when Efrem left. Irene commented, "He needs a woman to help him blow off some of that steam." She sashayed over to the rack to re-hang some newly pressed garments from the back.

Margot eyed her. "Careful with the comments, Irene. That's your co-worker Betty's friend you're talking about."

Irene replied back. "Well, Betty's not here right now to hear me and I'm just stating a fact. Someone needs to teach his wife how to unwind that man or he needs to find someone who will, that's all."

Realizing that sometimes ignoring Irene was the best way to calm down the scene, everyone went back to their tasks at hand. As the day progressed, Margot went through her notes with Marjorie and they sorted out the work for the week. There were some custom orders, including a mother of the groom dress for a Santa Lucia newcomer, Mrs. Jane Peacock. The staff had just recently begun to assemble the shift dress and bolero jacket in light blue wool crepe after the dress lining had been fitted to her. Marjorie and Margot organized the newly confirmed orders and floor stock for the Holiday

Soiree line. Margot left Marjorie to confer with her staff and continued remerchandising the returned garments and accessories onto the sales floor with Daphne.

Two-thirty came and went. There was no call from Tina Burbank. Although the staff was busy with their tasks, at about a quarter to three, it became difficult to concentrate. Daphne was just about to call the Burbank household when the phone rang in her hand. Immediately relieved, she picked it up.

"So do you have it?" pleaded a breathless man stating no introduction.

"Efrem, is that you?"

"Of course, it is. Are they there, the Burbanks? Did they bring the necklace?"

"No, now calm down, we haven't heard from them." Although she was anxious to get the matter resolved too, his panic was getting on her nerves. "It's not even three yet. I'll give her a few more minutes and if Tina doesn't call, I'll try the house again. Maybe she's running late or the housekeeper forgot to give her the message. I'll let you know as soon as we have anything to tell you."

Right after Daphne set down the receiver, it rang again. "Good afternoon, Poppy Cove," she replied.

"Hello, this is Tina Burbank. May I speak with Daphne?"

"Yes, Tina, thank you for returning my call. There seems to be a problem with Nora's necklace from the fashion show on Saturday night. We need to talk to her. Is she available?"

"No, Nora's at the university. Monday's a full class load for her and then she has an extra study group in the evening. She won't be home until around nine or so. I hope it's nothing serious."

Being a life long Santa Lucia resident and aware of how gossip spread like wildfire, Daphne did not want to stir the pot and reveal that Efrem had made a mistake with Isaac's real jewels. It could damage his future reputation in town and tarnish Isaac's, not to mention their father/son-in-law relationship. She wanted to resolve the matter in person, hopefully not even revealing the true problem to the Burbanks. She remained collected and inquired, "Could you possibly bring Nora's necklace to Poppy Cove this afternoon?"

"Oh, no, I don't think I can, dear. I believe Nora's got it in her jewelry box in her room and she's taken to locking her door when she's not home. Edward and I can't go in there when she's not here," Tina remarked.

Daphne was taken aback by the response. "Why would she do that?"

Tina laughed. "Well, she is nineteen years old and a college sophomore. We felt she was entitled to a little privacy."

Locking her bedroom door never occurred to Daphne. Although she was twenty-five years old, she still lived in her parents' home, estate actually. Her room, or *rooms* were always regarded with a healthy dose of respect as her private domain, as was the rest of her family's. Except from her younger sister Lizzy, who had lately felt the need to traipse in whenever the whim took her without knocking. "There is a matter with the necklace that we need to attend to as soon as possible. Not to cause any worry, but do you feel that it is safe in her room?"

"Well, the last I saw of it was early Sunday morning when we all came home from the ball. I helped her undress and we hid it away in her dresser."

"Okay, can you see if you or Nora could bring it by tomorrow at nine?"

"I think so. I'll check with Nora when she gets in, but it shouldn't be a problem," Tina paused. "Is everything all right, I mean with the necklace? It's not going to do her any harm or anything is it? Will it turn her neck green or leave a skin condition of some sort?"

Daphne smiled over the phone and thought quickly for a plausible reason. "No, nothing like that. Efrem just wants to check the settings and would like to take care of it here. Isaac's very fussy about the quality of Efrem's work and he would just feel more comfortable checking it privately, without Isaac giving his apprentice son-in-law a hard time, that's all." Daphne was quite proud of herself for coming up with a decent white lie that couldn't hurt anyone, even though it was something she didn't do often. Well, not too often, anyway.

The ladies rang off, settling for the morning. Daphne turned to Margot who was retagging some of the garments. "That's that. I don't think Efrem will be too pleased but honestly, it's the best we can do." She picked up the receiver and called Mendelson's. Efrem picked up on the first ring.

After their initial greeting, he pounced, "Is it there?"

"No, Efrem. They can't make it until the morning, but it will be here at nine."

Efrem blew off a steam of pressure. "Tomorrow? Can't we get it tonight?"

Daphne remained calm. "No. They can't arrange it."

"What's their address? I'll go get it myself."

His response riled Daphne and she tried to keep him rational. "Actually, it's safely locked up in Nora's room with no one knowing that anything is wrong. Try to relax, Efrem. Does Isaac know what's going on?"

"No, I don't think so," he admitted and replied quietly. "I've been keeping him busy by getting him to show me his catalogues of settings and watch parts. He's getting ready to leave for the day now."

Daphne brightened, "Well, then, you have nothing to worry about. The necklace is secure. Why don't you take the replica out of the safe after Isaac goes, then in the morning you can come by here and switch the pieces before you go to the shop? I doubt he'll be any the wiser."

Efrem's panic grew and he hissed a list of conclusions, including, "What if he shows up before me and sees that it's gone?"

"Honestly, how likely is that?"

"I don't care about the odds; I want this taken care of tonight. Give me their telephone number and address so I can find them." In his intensity, Efrem was losing his sense of propriety.

The conversation was getting more heated than Daphne appreciated or was used to dealing with. Through her discomfort, she maintained her friendly poise. "Now, Efrem, their telephone number and residential address are not listed. Do try to relax. They'll be here tomorrow and all will be well. You'll see."

"If you don't want to give it to me, I'll look in our records and see if we have their address in our client files. I want to fix this now!"

"I would strongly advise against that, Efrem. Look, you're new here and that's not how things are done with our set. Maybe in Los Angeles that's the way it would be handled, but you don't want to burn any bridges for yourself."

Efrem mumbled a noncommittal answer and hung up. Daphne felt rung out. "I hope he calms down and doesn't bother them tonight." She was fully aware that both Irene and Margot had kept pace with the conversation.

"Look, he's a friend of Betty's, right? And he's no tough guy, trust me, I know." Irene raised an eyebrow. "That group is such a bunch of sissies. They're too busy trying to kiss up to each other. He'll back down once he realizes that it'll hurt his future business."

Although what she said was crass, Daphne could see her point. "I hope you're right. If he does calm down, at least the necklace will be safe overnight." She changed tack and turned to Margot. "What do you make of the fact that Nora locks her room when she's not home? Don't you find that odd?"

Margot thought for a moment and considered Daphne's point of view. Margot was the same age as Daphne and had been living on her own for more than three years, only sharing living quarters with Mr. Cuddles, her striped tabby. She adored having her own little Santa Lucia bungalow and enjoyed the company of her man Tom when his busy schedule permitted. "What does Tina think of that?"

"Not much. She thinks that as a college girl she's entitled to her privacy."

"Tina is her mother," Margot reasoned. "She's probably right and Nora's not given her parents reasons to think there's anything wrong with that." Margot laughed at her friend's innocently quizzical look at the idea of wanting to keep a locked door in her own house. "A young woman's entitled to a little mystery."

Daphne shrugged. "I guess it never crossed my mind to keep secrets."

Irene sneered under her breath as she had her head down reconciling the last of the fashion show inventory list. "Maybe that's her secret. Daphne Huntington-Smythe—an open book with nothing written on the pages."

"Irene, I heard that! Really," Margot chided, stopping herself from laughing. She didn't think Daphne heard, thank goodness. She had to admit sometimes Irene's acerbic comments were pretty witty, but they were cutting. Luckily, she knew her audience and was very good with the customers. She could charm their clients, sharing the right amount of peppery gossip with the right people. In turn, the patrons rewarded Poppy Cove with regular, high-end purchases. It didn't hurt either that with her raven hair and svelte figure; Irene was a real looker in the clothes.

Irene sighed, glanced at the clock and closed the ledger. "Well, that's it. I'm done for the day."

"Thank you for coming in. It was appreciated," Margot commented. She made a note of the extra time all of the girls had put in over the weekend to help out. And also to discuss with Daphne a bonus for everyone after they worked out the profits from the show and subsequent orders. She pulled a gray wool crepe pencil skirt and red blouse with a bow at the neck in Irene's size off the rack that would show off her shapely figure and handed them to her. "Here's something from the new collection for you to wear tomorrow."

"Great! I will." When the store was open and the girls were working, they all wore garments from the sales floor. It was Poppy Cove's best form of advertising.

Shortly after Irene left, the girls had finished organizing and tidying the store. By five o'clock, all the staff, including Marjorie and the production team were ready to call it a day. Exhausted, Daphne and Margot were the last to leave. They turned off the lights and locked the door.

CHAPTER THREE

Daphne and Margot met on the front step of the shop on Tuesday morning. "I expected to see Efrem waiting for us," Margot stated.

"Me too. He was so eager. I hope he didn't go over to the Burbanks last night." Daphne got out her key from her patent black leather handbag and unlocked the door. "Speaking of which, Tina and Nora should be here any moment as well."

Margot flipped on the lights. "I'm sure once he gave it some thought he calmed down. Everything was safe, so realistically, it didn't matter if the necklaces were switched last night or this morning."

Daphne wedged the door open while Margot greeted the sewing staff as they came in for work and settled into their places in the back room. She heard the click of heels and glanced over her shoulder. Betty had an extra shift this week as well. She normally worked Thursday to Saturday, Poppy Cove's busiest days, but the owners felt the shop would be busy after the show. "Morning, Betty."

"Oh, I'm all right, I guess," she sighed fretfully, not paying attention to the greeting, which wasn't like Betty. Usually she was very bright and perky, but today she seemed deflated and wilted. Even though she was robed in a copper-colored day dress from the new fall collection that set off her blonde hair and blue eyes, she looked faded.

Margot and Daphne passed a look. Then Margot asked, "What's wrong, Betty?"

"I'm fine, but Rebecca called me late last night. Around midnight, I think. Dwight and I were already asleep."

Daphne opened her mouth and was ready to rush headlong into the conversation. Margot touched her arm, silently indicating she wanted to take the lead on this line of questioning. If it was slowly and casually brought up, they weren't sure how much Betty might reveal about the necklace, if she knew anything at all. The cool-headed brunette continued while Daphne listened eagerly. "Really? Why did she do that?"

Betty looked around the empty room. It was early and no customers had come in yet and the rest of the staff was busy in the back. It was just the three of them in hearing distance and Betty wasn't good at keeping things inside. She spoke in a hushed tone, peppered with a sense of panic, "I don't know if I should say this, but Efrem didn't come home from work yesterday."

"Is that usual for him?"

"No, not at all!" Betty exclaimed. "They've only been married for six months. Rebecca says they've not even had a dinner apart!" Betty looked beseechingly at the storeowners, hoping they'd come up with a possibly harmless and reasonable explanation. "She's worried he's cheating on her already! You don't think he would, do you?" Betty crumpled into one of the lounge chairs near the fitting rooms.

Margot came over to the seating area and sat down beside her. She thought before she spoke and then proceeded carefully. "Probably not, not so soon after the marriage. Unless Rebecca had cause to think there was another woman?" Both Margot and Daphne shared her sense of anxiety, but for other reasons that they did not feel at liberty to discuss with her yet. They'd rather hear Betty bring up the necklace mix-up. That way they were still keeping their word to Efrem.

"I don't know. He doesn't seem like the type. When we were out on Saturday night he was devoted to her," Betty continued. "He didn't even turn his gaze to another woman, including the beautiful pageant girls who were swarming all over the place, especially that Mary Ann. Unlike Dwight, but he's just a gawker, he doesn't do anything about it, so I don't mind." Betty shook her head. "Efrem was really good to her when he found out her mother had died."

Rebecca had been through a lot when she moved away. Miriam, Rebecca's mother, had always been weak and sickly. But four years ago, when her mother truly became ill with cancer, her parents decided to hide the seriousness of it from her. They sent her away to Los Angeles to start her own life, living with Isaac's younger sister, Rose.

Aunt Rose lived a glamorous life in the city. She was a single career woman working in the Finer Dresses Department of the Beverly Hills Robinsons-May and was more than happy to take her niece under her wing, away from her sick and dying mother. The family shielded Rebecca from the worst of her mother's illness and kept her occupied with print and department store modeling, while forming a respectable social life of parties and dating with members of their neighborhood synagogue on Fairfax. Shortly after her Miriam's death, she met Efrem at a friend's wedding. He was a well-respected young man, the son of an established jeweler in the district. Her own feelings of grief gave her the desire to marry and make her own family. This fine young man was just the right combination of new love and familiar ways. It was clear after she introduced her beau to her father that he could easily become the son he never had, taking over the business as Isaac was getting weary and considering retirement.

It didn't seem that Betty or Rebecca, for that matter, had any knowledge about the situation with the necklaces or that Efrem had been at Poppy Cove yesterday. Margot suggested, "Maybe he was working late. We had a lot of orders that came in from the fashion show, so maybe Mendelson's did, too?"

"Sometimes he might be late coming home from work, but he'll always call and Rebecca will hold dinner for him, but last night he didn't."

"When did he show up?"

"He never did! I called Rebecca at seven this morning and she was in such a state. He never came home. She's not heard from him at all, tried calling him at the store when he was late and there was no answer. She doesn't want to call Isaac because she doesn't want her father to think there may be problems in the marriage, but she probably will and if he doesn't know anything, she's going to call the police and report him as missing. What if something really bad has happened?"

"Yeah, three sheets happened," came a sultry voice through the front door.

Everyone turned to look at Irene who'd slinked in, looking devilishly attractive in her new gray skirt and red blouse. She had matched them with jet-black beads and patent leather pumps. "You are talking about Efrem, right?" she continued.

Betty sat up and brightened. "Yes! Did you see him?"

"Oh yeah, I saw him."

"Where? When?"

"At Bud's, near the rails," Irene mentioned a dive bar in the industrial area of town, between the railroad tracks and the interstate freeway. It was an area of town where none of the other girls frequented or had any knowledge of. Daphne had only passed by it on the freeway and never had crossed into it.

Betty asked innocently, "What were you doing there?"

"Eddie. He's got an in with the owner. He runs a craps game at the back table and we get free drinks."

Daphne jumped in. "I thought you rejected him on Saturday night."

Irene shrugged and took a sip of her coffee from the cup she brought in with her. "That was just for Saturday."

Betty remarked, "I don't know what you see in him."

Irene took another sip of coffee and set her drink down on the counter. "Aw, he's a bit of a runt, but he's all right, good for a laugh. Besides, he always picks up the tab and knows a lot of people. He might be my ticket to a more exciting ride. It's better going out with him than sitting at my Grandmother's every evening." She was the same age as Betty, but with a far different upbringing. She grew up in Los Angeles and after a few wild and adventurous years in her late teens, she was sent to live with her father's mother, a woman in her early eighties, who didn't press for too much information and chose to ignore her when she saw Irene sneak out of her bedroom late at night.

Daphne was more interested in what happened with Efrem than Irene's love life and steered the conversation in that direction. "Do you know why Efrem was there? Was he with anyone?"

Irene had her head down, looking through the appointment book. "He was sitting at the bar with that letch, Dirk Roberts."

"I didn't know they knew each other," Daphne remarked. "What were they doing?"

Betty sat up straighter. Both Margot and she swiveled in their seats to pay attention to Irene's reply. "Drinking. Seriously drinking."

"Well, yes, we understand that, but anything else, talking? Could you hear what they were saying?" Daphne tried to move the conversation along.

"They'd been there awhile by the time I got there, so it was pretty slurry. Dirk was going on about his ex, Kitty, and how if he had the dough, he could win her back. Efrem was going on about something he had to fix. He had something in his hands, kept fiddling with it and Dirk kept trying to grab at it, but kept missing. They were so far gone they weren't really listening to each other, just talking out loud in turns," she shook her head and chuckled about their problems."

A feminine blur rushed by the store's Cove Street picture window, followed by a loping gangly male. "Was that Loretta and Jake?" Daphne questioned. She poked her head out of the doorway. "Loretta, thanks for the write-up yesterday. Hey, where are you off to in such a hurry? What's going on?"

Loretta practically skidded to a stop. She turned her small bird-like frame around and answered Daphne. "Thanks, you earned it! Sorry, don't have time to talk. Something's happened at the Burbank's. Weathers' been there for the last hour," she said, referring to the paper's crime reporter. "I'm going to see if there's anything I can use for my column. After all, if something happened at the home of the reigning Miss Santa Lucia, there's got to be a story for our social set. I'll fill you in later!" Loretta and Jake continued at their pace to the next block where they got into her big dark green Buick and sped off.

Margot sat up straighter in her chair and looked at Daphne. "Did I hear right? Michael Weathers is at the Burbank's?"

"Yes! What do you think happened?" Daphne's eyes grew wide. "You don't think this has anything to do with Efrem and the necklace, do you?"

Betty piped up, "What do you mean? Why would Efrem have anything to do with the Burbanks? And what's this about a necklace?"

The two shop owners faced each other and made a silent agreement to fill Betty in on what they knew of Efrem, the necklace and the Burbanks.

CHAPTER FOUR

After Betty was caught up and Irene's information was absorbed, the staff was at a loss with what to think or do. All the girls in their own way started fussing around with details, just to keep their minds and hands busy. Margot and Daphne retreated up the wrought iron spiral staircase to their private office with full intentions to work on ordering supplies for the post-fashion show rush, but as they settled down to their desks, they ended up talking about the current events.

"I guess that means that Tina and Nora won't be coming this morning," Margot stated the obvious, but putting it into words somehow opened the door for speculation.

"I sure wonder what happened at the Burbank's. I'm really worried. I mean, the police, crime reporter...and Efrem missing." Daphne flipped through an accessories catalogue, then looked across at Margot, who had her head down looking at taffeta swatches. "Say, do you think you could give..."

"No! I can't." Margot knew exactly where she was going.

"Oh, come on, I'm sure you could."

"No."

"Flirt a little. Pretend to be calling to ask him out for lunch. He loves it when you make plans for him. And, in the course of conversation, you find out what's going on, well, that's just how that happens." Daphne was referring to Margot's boyfriend, Tom, the Santa Lucia Police Detective.

Margot had to admit she was curious and he would probably have the answers, but he didn't like her meddling in his work, just as much as she didn't like his advice on fabrics, considering he was a little colorblind. She shook the idea out of her head. "No, he hates it when I ask him questions about work. Look what happened last time." Margot was referring back to a couple of weeks ago when they became involved in solving the murder of their friend and client, Constance Stearns-Montgomery.

"Yes, that's exactly my point! By you sharing what you knew with Tom, you saved my life!" Daphne paused. "Did you say anything to Tom last night about Efrem's visit yesterday?"

"No, I didn't think there was anything to say about it at the time." Margot thought a little longer about the latest developments. "Maybe I should say something now. I don't want to get Efrem into trouble, but with him not coming home last night, and something happening at the Burbank's, it sounds like Tom might need to know about his visit yesterday." She picked up the receiver and dialed his direct line that she knew by heart.

The phone rang five times and then double jingled, which meant it was routed to the main switchboard. "Santa Lucia Police Department, Detective Malone's line. How may I help you?" A pleasant female voice answered the call.

"Oh, hello. This is Margot Williams calling for Tom. Is he available?"

"Margot? Hi, it's Penny! How are you?" Penny Garrett was a pleasant young woman and a regular shopper at Poppy Cove.

"Fine, thanks. Listen, I was trying to reach Tom. Is he available?"

There was a slight pause as Penny looked at the in and out board. "Gee, no, I'm sorry, he's out on a call."

Margot felt her breath catch, followed by a sinking feeling. She started gently prodding. "Oh, something happen?"

Penny hesitated, but replied in a whisper. She loved a good scoop like any other operator. "Yes! But I can't tell you."

"You can't?" Margot played along. Daphne no longer pretended to be working and blatantly followed the conversation.

"No, but if you guess, I can't tell a lie..." Penny prompted.

Margot pursued. "Okay. Would this have anything to do with the Burbanks?"

Penny was astonished at how fast she'd put it together. "How did you know?"

"Oh, a little bird told me." She grinned to herself when she thought about Loretta, with her birdlike features and the way she darted about.

"Hmm. Well, do you need to reach Tom? Do you want me to radio him or leave a message for him to call you when he gets back to the station?"

"No Penny, it's okay. Chances are he won't be available for lunch today, anyway. If something big has happened."

She agreed. "It's something big, all right. He'll be tied up all day."

"Really? What exactly is going on, Penny?"

Penny nervously coughed, feeling she'd revealed enough. "Sorry, Margot. Got to go. Chief's line is lighting up." With that, she abruptly disconnected the call.

"Well, what did she say?" Daphne eagerly questioned her as she hung up the phone.

Margot sighed. "Sounds like Tom's been called to the Burbank's as well."

Daphne gave a low whistle. "Wow! It must be serious then." She drummed her fingers on her desk. "Did she tell you anything else?"

"No, not really; just that he'll be busy all day." Margot straightened up her papers. "Right, then we're not going to find anything out at the moment. We might as well get back to work ourselves. Lord knows we've got a lot to do." Margot turned on the radio, filling the air with jazz from a Los Angeles station, determined that the modern sounds would distract their racing minds.

Daphne had a little trouble settling in. Her thoughts continued to go to what was now looking like a crime scene. What exactly happened and who was involved? Eventually she did focus on filling her orders for the trinkets and baubles she needed to stock for the holiday season. In addition to the pageant queen's necklace from Mendelson's, Poppy Cove had featured big, bold gems of ruby, emerald, amethyst and diamond-like large clear glass and pearls in the show. Daphne wanted to make sure they had plenty of goodies for their clients. Some of her favorites were a pair of flower earrings made of oblong colored petals, with a large pale green peridot-like glass gem in the center and smaller green glass stones at the end of each petal point. She also favored a large amethyst piece made into a choker on a dark purple velvet ribbon. Before long, she was happily absorbed in the bright cheery bracelets, necklaces, brooches and clip-on earrings.

Margot was looking over her orders from the show and stock levels. Yesterday, Marjorie had given her an estimate of the notions—buttons, zippers, thread, tulle, grosgrain, horsehair binding, boning, all the things that made the dresses take shape and flatter a woman's curvy figure or restrain any extra added padding a woman may naturally have. So absorbed were they in their work, Daphne actually jumped in her seat when Irene buzzed from downstairs to let them know that their eleven o'clock appointment, Mrs. Jane Peacock, had arrived for her fitting.

Daphne and Margot made their way downstairs to greet their client. Betty had seated her in the dressing room area and had been joined by Marjorie who had brought out her dress from the back workroom. Mrs. Peacock was a recent Santa Lucian who had moved with her husband, Herbert, from Portland, Oregon, when he became a history teacher at the new Stearns Academy for girls. Their son, Robert, was getting married to his sweetheart Susie in Texas on December 28th in a small but semi-formal event. To celebrate the occasion, Jane had decided to splurge on having a dress made rather than making it herself. After all, she was only going to be the mother of the groom once. This was Jane's first fitting of the overall garment. Hopefully, if it went well, all they would need to do is confirm the hem length and the ensemble would be ready in plenty of time before the wedding, with little or no fuss.

Mrs. Peacock was in her late forties, with graying hair, a bit plumpish, but with a delightful smile and sparkling light blue eyes. The dress was in an icy blue wool crepe, sleeveless and cut on the bias, draping beautifully from the bodice below the bust in a gentle A-line silhouette to just below the knee. The matching bolero jacket was to have small rhinestone buttons and Daphne had suggested a smart pillbox hat, clutch purse and gloves.

Jane stepped out of the dressing room and into the stage area wearing her complete outfit, from hat to shoes for the first time, beaming and walking as if she were on a cloud. "Oh, ladies, I am so pleased!" She gave a little twirl.

Marjorie, a stickler for detail, gave a small frown and rushed over, noticing that the lining was a little longer than the dress on the right side. Jane stopped abruptly as Marjorie took a couple of pins out of her mouth, adjusted the hem and stepped back. "Now that's better." Then she smiled.

Jane looked toward Margot and Daphne for their approval. "Well, what do you think?"

"I'll take it," came a voice off from the side.

Margot turned around to look and saw a familiar customer walking towards the group from the sales floor. "Can I help you, Mrs. Marshall?"

"Yes, this dress here. If this woman isn't going to buy it, I will." Mrs. Marshall, who was a regular shopper at the store had a habit of wanting any garment that wasn't readily available, such as outfits on the mannequins that would not be removed until a week or two later or sample items that were not yet for sale. That included custom apparel that was made for others and she simply must have them right away, not willing to go through a fitting procedure or willing to pay for the extra work of tailoring special pieces that custom apparel required.

"Mrs. Marshall, I'd be happy to discuss making you a garment if you would like to book an appointment. Irene can help you set up a time." Margot gestured toward the direction of the sales desk where Irene was finishing up another purchase.

The demanding customer huffed and turned on her heel, clutching one of the first items she saw, a green day dress that was, thank God, in her size and suited her coloring. "No, I'll just take this," and walked over to Irene.

The shop owners smirked at the unusual but expected behavior from the woman and turned their attention back to Mrs. Peacock. "Jane, you look lovely. If you're not careful, your Herbert's going to mistake you for the bride!" Daphne complimented.

Margot couldn't help but smile and take a sense of pride in her work. Jane did look beautiful—smart, sophisticated and in no way dowdy or frumpy, which could easily happen with women of a certain age and build. "You make the dress come to life, Jane." She paused, letting her take in feeling good for a moment. "There're just one or two little things we need to adjust."

Jane stood still while Marjorie and Margot conferred off to the side. The hem was then pinned, the buttons and buttonholes marked for placement and a slight adjustment again to the right armhole. "That'll do it. We'll have it ready for you to pick up in say, three weeks? You're not in a hurry, are you? We've got quite a few items on the go from the fashion show."

"That's plenty of time, thank you. How did the show go?" Jane and her Herbert were of modest means, and lived contentedly in the teachers' housing on the school grounds. Yacht clubs and charity balls were not part of their social circle. They were much more the type of folk to spend a Saturday evening playing cards, eating sandwiches and drinking beer than swilling champagne cocktails at swanky social clubs.

"Really well, thank you. We've been taking plenty of bookings and have had lots of interest in the new items." Margot looked around the shop and noticed for the first time that day that the sales floor was quite busy with customers flipping through the racks, commenting about the garments and such.

Daphne had brought over a couple of necklaces and showed them to Jane. One in particular, a rhinestone number that was similar to the buttons on the jacket caught Jane's fancy. "I like that one. May I try it on?" Daphne fastened it around her neck and stood back to have a look, nodding with approval. "Sold!" Jane confirmed.

Marjorie suggested, "Mrs. Peacock, why don't we get you changed and I'll take your items to the back with me." Betty assisted Jane in the fitting room and handed the work in progress to the head seamstress and the accessories to Daphne to store until the final fitting. Margot looked over the schedule and arranged for an appointment in three weeks, handing over a card to Jane.

Once she was back in her original clothes, the girls asked her how things were going for her and her Herbert. "Well, we're settling in. Of course, I'm sure it would have been different had Mrs. Stearns-Montgomery not died, but we have to admit that Headmistress Larsen runs a tight ship. She may be strict, but she's leaving my Herbert alone to do his job."

"And the wedding plans? All going according to schedule?" Margot inquired.

"Oh, yes. Being that the wedding is in Texas, Susie is living there with her parents until then. She and her mother are really taking care of the whole affair. We'll be going just before Christmas and staying until New Year's. We'll be more involved when we get there." She sighed a little wistfully, giving the indication that she wished that she were more active in the planning, as Robert is her only child. "Well, at least they'll be settling in Portland. Robert is taking after his father and has now confirmed his teaching post at a high school there."

After Jane left, the rest of the day progressed in a blur. The shop was busy with the society ladies coming in to look at the fashion show apparel in person and a couple of other fittings and appointments. There was a constant hum of the machines and presses from the back creating new garments, but it was low in volume compared to the gossipy murmurs from the clientele. Nobody had any truthful information about the situation, but everyone had a point of view or opinion of what was happening over at the Burbank's. According to the loudest talk, none of the family had been seen, but the police were crawling all over the house and yard. Also Dr. Burbank's dental office was closed and someone thought they might have seen an ambulance in the morning at the residence, but no one could be sure.

All the while, Betty had been nervously fussing and fretting whenever she didn't have a customer to help. Often she overheard snippets of gossip that she could possibly construe as evidence of Efrem's involvement. She was having a rough day—being more of a hindrance than help. She was mishanging dresses, skipping buttons, mixing up garments in the dressing room. Around 3:30, there was a telephone call for her. Daphne had picked it up and it was a young woman. She did not introduce herself and seemed in a panic. After Betty had spoken with her, she apologized to the shop owners and made a hasty early retreat out the door, leaving in tears. Daphne and Margot wondered if that had been Rebecca on the line and what had happened to make their exemplary employee leave so abruptly. They decided that they wouldn't dock her pay, as it wasn't in her nature to be flighty or dramatic.

CHAPTER FIVE

Loretta showed up around 4 p.m., wide-eyed and full of energy, living on adrenalin after the day's shocking events. "Girls!" She hissed, grabbing Daphne and Margot's elbows and guiding them to the stairs. "Boy, what I have to tell you!"

Startled, the pair looked at Loretta between them and let her move them towards the office. She looked back at Irene with a sharp stare. "I don't care how busy you get, we are not to be disturbed."

Margot glanced back over her shoulder, rolling her eyes to Irene, regaining co-owner authority over the business. The manager nodded nonchalantly, with understanding that no matter what that gossipmonger said, Poppy Cove business came first over small town fodder.

"Okay Loretta, what's this all about? Do you know what happened at the Burbank's?" Daphne asked as soon as they had made it upstairs and behind a closed door.

Loretta could barely sit in her lounge chair. She perched on the edge, ready to explode with everything she knew, regardless of the order of language. She took a shallow breath and launched in. "Nora's been murdered!"

"What?" Margot set down the kettle she was filling.

Loretta repeated the phrase again and continued. "The story's been put to the presses, so I can tell you now, but don't repeat it to anyone. I mean it—you have to pinky swear!" She held out her hand, and after a brief pause the girls realized she really meant it and obliged her. They huddled in a group as the Society Editor told them what she knew.

"Well," she paused for effect, knowing she had a captive audience. "When I got there, the place was crawling with cops, including your Tom and the Police Chief. Sometime during the night, someone broke into Nora's bedroom and bludgeoned her on the back of the head. Apparently, one good blow knocked her dead."

The room was silent while they took it all in. Margot and Daphne were breathlessly in shock after hearing the news. Loretta came down from her reporter instinct reactions. She started to feel a weary sadness as it sunk in that it wasn't just a news story, but the murder of a beautiful young girl with so much life ahead of her. For the first time that day, Loretta's guard came down and she began to cry.

Margot made herself busy by making tea while Daphne tidied up the papers on her desk, which gave their friend a chance to compose herself. When she calmed down to a low sniffle, Daphne gently inquired, "Honey, do you feel okay to tell us any more?"

Loretta sat up straighter, took a sip of her tea and turned towards Margot, "Do you have anything stronger?"

The girls smirked and knew she'd be okay. Daphne reached down to her bottom drawer and pulled out a bottle of brandy that they kept for just such an occasion. After she topped up her cup, Loretta took a longer sip, sighed and continued. "Here's what I can tell you. Sometime late last night, early morning, really, around 2 or 3 a.m., the police figure someone climbed through Nora's bedroom window. She was startled awake and as she woke up, the murderer used her Miss Santa Lucia scepter and hit her. She wasn't found until around 7:30 this morning."

"Didn't her parents hear anything when it happened?" Daphne asked.

"No. Her parents sleep on the other side of the house and from what the police told Weathers, it happened so fast that there wasn't much of a struggle, so they didn't hear anything. Her door was still locked. Whoever did it left through the window, the same way they came in. Apparently, all they had to do was pry it open a little wider to use it. Weathers finally got into the room around noon to have a look around and get a couple of photos that he could use. Being that it was just one hit, there wasn't a lot of blood and the scepter which they figure was the murder weapon was on the floor, right beside her bed." Loretta's report gave them all the shivers as they imagined the scene.

"Anyway, as I was saying, Tina got up as usual at seven and when Nora didn't come to breakfast by 7:30, she went to her bedroom door which was still locked. Then when she knocked on it and there was no answer she had Edward bust the door down. It must have been horrible for them. Dr. Browning had to give Tina a sedative to knock her out cold." Loretta paused and finished her tea. She held out her cup to Daphne. "Got any more?" Daphne gave her more brandy then looked at Margot, who shrugged and held out her cup. They all had a good dose.

"Do the police have any idea why this happened?" Margot ventured, cautiously. She had a foreboding, sinking feeling that somehow Efrem was involved. She certainly hoped her instincts were wrong, but she could tell by Daphne's silence that she was thinking that as well.

"It seems that the place had been ransacked, too. The police have a few theories, but won't confirm anything. At this point, they won't say if it was a robbery gone wrong or it was a cold-blooded murder made to look like a robbery. Not a lot was taken and although the one solid hit to her head was fatal and looked awful, there wasn't that much of a struggle. Whoever it was, when they used the scepter, they had gloves on so there aren't any fingerprints and the only clue they have is that the murderer cracked the window sash on the way out."

Daphne blurted out, wanting to know more. "You said that her room was ransacked. Was anything taken?"

"From what they can tell, just the necklace from the fashion show. You know, the replica of the Mendelson's piece."

Daphne let out a puff of air. "That's not good news."

"No, it isn't, but they have a suspect already in custody."

Margot gulped and then asked the question. "Who?"

"Efrem Goldberg." Loretta reported. "He was found parked a block away. Passed out, sleeping, dead drunk with the necklace in his hands."

Daphne and Margot exchanged looks. "What?" Loretta asked, her eyes widened. "You two know something!"

No one said a word. Loretta continued. "Oh, come on, spill it! I told you things that could get me fired. What do you have?"

Finally after a long pause, Daphne said, "Loretta, this is so far off the record, you can't repeat this. No way."

She jumped up off her chair and perched herself on Daphne's desk. "I'm all ears, lips sealed," as she made a lock and key motion.

Margot interjected here and there filling in the gaps as Daphne told their friend about the necklace, Efrem, how he was seen at Bud's and never came home last night.

"Wow!" she exhaled. "That sounds bad. I never would have taken him for the murdering type. I mean, we don't know him well, but still he seemed to be a pretty nice and down to earth guy. I was shocked when I found out he was near the scene and arrested, but this just makes it worse."

"I thought he was one of the good ones, too," Margot agreed. "You should have seen him, though. He was really desperate yesterday, irrational. And then he didn't come home, got drunk at a dive bar…I guess you never know."

Daphne nodded. "That phone call for Betty must have been from Rebecca! Poor girl, no wonder she was so upset. To think they all went out on Saturday after the show and had a really nice time."

"Well, they're not having such a nice time now." Loretta surmised. "He sure looks guilty." Loretta thought for a moment in the silent room. Her expression changed quickly, her brainwaves practically audible. "Irene said that she thought she saw Efrem with the necklace at Bud's, right?" Her audience nodded.

"What do you mean?" Daphne felt a little perplexed. With so much going on, it was getting harder to keep score. Then the light bulb went on in her head. "Why is there only one necklace?"

Margot caught onto the chain of thought and started pacing, vocalizing the realization. "So he just had one, right?"

"Yes," Loretta confirmed.

"Which one? The real or the replica?" Margot pursued.

Loretta thought for a moment. "To be honest, I don't think anyone was questioning if it was a real or a fake piece. At that point, the cops assumed it was the stolen one and evidence of the crime just committed. Efrem was too groggy to say much. He just mumbled and clutched the one in his hand as they poured him into the police car."

"And the other wasn't found, either at the Burbank's or with Efrem?"

"Not from what I know."

"So," Margot deduced. "If Efrem had the replica, he may be innocent. It would mean that he hadn't broken in and stole the necklace from the Burbank's."

"But," Loretta picked up the theory. "If he has the real one, it looks like he's guilty as sin."

"I better call Tom. He needs to know about this. He must be back by now. If not, I'll leave an urgent message for him." Margot picked up the receiver and started to dial.

"But you're forgetting something," Daphne stated. "There's still only one necklace."

Loretta was flummoxed. "I don't get it."

Margot put the phone down, wanting to think through what they had concluded. "So what really happened? If Efrem had the real necklace, he would be the one who broke in and swapped them out, but there would be the replica left there. The police said that there wasn't a necklace present and therefore they assumed it had been stolen during the break-in."

Daphne shrugged. "Maybe he panicked and didn't swap them."

Margot made her point again. "So where is the other necklace, then? Real or fake?" She turned to Loretta. "They only found one with him, right?"

Loretta nodded firmly. "Yes, the police confirmed that. Weathers was able to quote them."

She began pacing again to work out the theories as it was becoming clearer the more they went over it. "But if he still had the fake, that means that he didn't break in or kill Nora."

Daphne interjected. "Which means that possibly someone else knew that Nora had the real necklace and stole it, then murdered her to get away with the valuable piece!"

Loretta added another theory. "And before Efrem was found in his car there was buzz around town that Miss Mary Ann Rutherford was quite envious of Nora for receiving it. They had a bit of a tiff on Saturday night about it, didn't they?"

The girls had forgotten all about that. Daphne felt a rush of relief that Efrem may not be involved after all, but a titch ashamed to be thinking poorly of a young lady. "So do we think she's a suspect?"

"A possible one," Loretta confirmed. "Jealousy's a strong motive for murder. She may have been the one to sneak in and take it, not knowing or even caring if it was real or fake. It was Nora's and Mary Ann wanted it."

"So, if that's the case," Margot expanded, "it's not about the real or fake gems, but Mary Ann's resentful rage."

"It could be," Loretta supposed. "After all, the blow that killed Nora wasn't done by brute strength. It was more the power of the scepter, the angle of the hit and the element of surprise that did her in. A girl of Mary Ann's build could have done that if so inclined."

Daphne shook her blonde curls. "I don't know. This is too much. You'd better tell Tom all you know and let the police department handle it."

The ladies all agreed, took another nip of brandy and Margot called Tom. After she told him all she knew, the lovebirds exchanged their terms of endearments followed by a stern warning from Tom in his official capacity to tell her to stay out of police business, while Daphne and Loretta listened in and snickered to each other.

It was already after five and the staff downstairs was closing up shop. Irene called up and let them know that she and everyone else were leaving for the day. The three sat there, a little warm from the brandy and feeling at loose ends. Margot's beau was tied up with obviously murderous work, Loretta's column was in and Daphne had no plans with Daniel, or anyone else for that matter. The three decided to have dinner at Antonio's, a restaurant just down the way.

CHAPTER SIX

Margot locked the shop's front door behind them and dropped the key in her small, patent black leather purse. They looked out onto the picturesque fountain of Avila Square. Dating back to the 1700's, it was the true heart of downtown and one of the few structures that survived the devastating 1922 earthquake. Lovingly restored during the following rebuilding phase, it remained the main focal and gathering point of the town.

The ladies strolled down Cove Street. It was a beautiful evening in early October and the sun was getting lower in the sky. The days had been warm and dry, but the evenings were a little cooler with the fog holding off at bay on the ocean. The main street ran down to the wharf and the waterfront providing a spectacular view. Before long, they reached the sweet little Italian restaurant, Antonio's.

The place had been there for many years. It was a quaint hot spot that all of them often frequented, run by Antonio and Maria Chelli. Antonio himself met the ladies at the door. "Ah, what a pleasure! Three of my most favorite beauties visiting me all at once," the affectionate man effused. Although he was middle aged, balding with a slightly rotund waistline from all the good food and happy living, he still exuded the genuine charm of a true ladies' man. Devoted to his wife, but appreciative of the fairer sex, the girls responded to his kisses and hugs warmly. "Where shall you sit? Outside, inside?"

They looked over at the loggia that was lovely with vines displaying big, plump grapes dripping all over in bunches and huge green leaves with fairy lights. The sight was heavenly, but the fresh sea air was beginning to feel cool. They made a quick consensus to sit inside.

Antonio led them past the bar to a cozy booth against the brick wall, but not far from the action of full tables and noisy atmosphere filled with plenty of laughter, song and wine flowing. In their space they could comfortably conspire about the case. The tables had red and white checked tablecloths and Chianti bottle candles. The brick trim and wood plank floors with plenty of leafy, sprawling green plants and colorful travel and food posters decorating the walls made it very charming and homey. Here and there were black and white photos, proudly displayed in wooden frames showing generations of the Chelli family back in Italy, working, celebrating and living their lives.

"I bring martinis first, menus later?" Antonio smiled slyly. He knew his clientele well. The girls grinned and nodded. The drinks arrived shortly and after a quick sip, the scheming began.

Daphne spoke first in an eager voice just above a whisper. "What do you think really happened?"

"Well, let's consider all we can." Loretta said as she got out her notebook, while Margot thoughtfully ran her finger around the rim of her glass. Each had their own ways of deducing theories. Daphne rambled out loud, Loretta wrote out notes, Margot got lost in thought.

Daphne continued. "There seemed to be a lot of strange behavior last night. I mean, Efrem out on a bender, making friends with Dirk, found near the scene of the crime with a necklace and of course, poor Nora being killed. I still can't see Efrem as a murderer, though."

"But what about Mary Ann? Could she really be that vicious?" Margot questioned.

Loretta's pencil stopped moving and she had her familiar 'cat ate the canary' look on her face. "Well, I did overhear a couple of other things from the police before they found Efrem's car..." she trailed off.

Margot leaned in closer while Daphne was all ears. She exclaimed, "Fess up, Loretta. What else did you hear?"

The reported turned coy, pulling back a little. "Oh, I don't know if I should say anything, just hearsay, really. It may not be anything and I don't have the whole picture." She loved reeling them in like fish on a hook.

The girls had known Loretta long enough to know she liked to tease out her scoops, but eventually always told them everything. Daphne continued in the game. "Come on, you've been dying to tell us all along."

Loretta looked for an encouraging nod from Margot and then she knew she had her friends enthralled. "Well, I told you about Mary Ann being jealous and all."

"Yes, and?" Daphne made a motion as she spoke, trying to move the reporter along.

The girls stopped talking as Luigi, Antonio's son and best waiter, brought over menus. They greeted him briefly and resumed their conversation. "I overheard the police questioning Tina about Nora's social life and when they mentioned the possibility that she had a boyfriend, Tina got all uptight and said that no, she had been seeing someone, but they made sure that it was over."

"What did that mean?" Daphne pursued as Margot pensively listened.

"Okay, so what I could gather when the detectives asked her to elaborate, Nora had been seeing someone in the summer, but her parents didn't like him. Thought he wasn't right for Nora and had encouraged her to break up with him when college resumed. Tina was sure she had."

Margot chimed in. "Had she?"

"The police weren't so sure. They asked the Burbanks about her bedroom door being locked and apparently Nora started to lock it around the time when they asked her to stop seeing him."

"Who was she dating?" Daphne asked.

"At first, Tina tried to avoid answering, saying that it was no longer an issue, so she didn't want to say, but when they pressed her for it, one of the rookie cops had dropped something in the bedroom and I couldn't hear anything," Loretta groaned. "I wasn't actually in the house. They wouldn't let me in so I was on the back patio. Weathers made it inside, but he was busy at the crime scene and missed it. He didn't hear that part of the conversation at all."

"So, there's another suspect," Daphne confirmed, as Luigi came by to take their orders. The girls guiltily looked over the menus quickly and decided on splitting the large cold antipasti platter with extra breadsticks and moved on to a carafe of the restaurant's house red made in central Italy from the Chelli family vineyards in the old country.

Margot spoke out loud what she'd been mulling over. "What about Dirk?"

Loretta looked over the top of her rhinestone cat-eye glasses. "What about him?"

"Irene was pretty sure that Efrem had a necklace at the bar and Dirk was trying to grasp it," Daphne recollected. "Say, you don't think he plied Efrem with drinks at the bar to get to the necklace? I mean what if maybe as Efrem drank, he told Dirk about the switch? If Dirk knew that he had the replica and that the real necklace was at the Burbanks, possibly he had a hand in the murder, or even did it?"

"Well, he was making comments at the fashion show about acquiring the necklace and how he couldn't afford it," Loretta added.

Daphne nodded. "Yes, and that he could possibly lure Kitty back with it!"

Loretta furiously scribbled on her notepad. "Oh yeah, that's good!"

"Also," Margot coolly brought up another angle. "Eddie actually fingered the necklace backstage and he was at the bar, too."

"And Irene was at the bar with Eddie," Daphne stated flatly.

"She had better not be tangled up in this," Margot gritted her teeth at the idea.

The food arrived and the girls realized how hungry they were. They took a break to eat. Everything tasted so good. Margot suddenly thought that with all that was going on, neither Daphne nor she had complimented Loretta properly on the fashion show write-up and photos in Monday's edition of the *Times*. It was well done with plenty of pictures that showed off the garments beautifully and featured some of their most prominent clients.

As she accepted their compliments, Loretta became sad thinking about the young girl featured on her society pages the day before. "You know, she looked just lovely," she sighed. "They wanted to use the picture again on the front page for tomorrow but at the last minute Jack, the Editor-in-Chief, decided on her pageant-winning picture instead. She was holding the scepter in it and he thought it would sell more copies."

Daphne was repulsed. "Ugh. Isn't that kind of morbid?"

Loretta shrugged and waved her fork in the air. "Hey, what sells papers is what he's interested in more than what's in good taste." She sat up straighter, craning her neck to look over to the bar and got excited. "There's Weathers. I'm going to see if he found out anything more. He was heading back over to the Police Station after we put the issue to bed to see what he could scout out."

As she got up, Margot grabbed her arm firmly. "Loretta, don't say anything about what we told you. Tom warned me to stay out of this! It's all speculation, not fact. He'd be mad if I did anything to mess up the case."

"Oh, tish-tosh! I won't say anything I shouldn't. I'll get *him* to blab. He loves to talk after I flatter him just that little bit." She smiled and patted Margot on the arm. "Just relax, you'll see."

The girls watched as Loretta made her way to the bar where Weathers was sitting with a buxom blonde in a cheap, too tight dress, definitely not from Poppy Cove. Daphne and Margot sat entranced as they watched Loretta laugh, pitch and flatter Michael and his date, then saw how he started talking, animated and running off at the mouth. A few minutes later, she came back to the table, pleased with herself.

"Well, anything new?" Daphne inquired.

"Yes. Efrem's still being questioned. He was so drunk last night, his story keeps changing and they can't get a full picture from him."

"That's not going to help him," Margot concluded.

Loretta nodded. "Not only that, but he had some minor abrasions on his forearms that could indicate that he'd been in a struggle, with a person or a window and sash, perhaps?" She paused and then had one more shoe to drop. "And, he was found with the fake necklace. They searched his car and that's all they found."

"Which means," Margot surmised, "Somebody else has the real one, and who would that be?"

"Possibly the killer," Daphne concluded.

CHAPTER SEVEN

Daphne had an uneasy night thinking about all the possibilities of Nora's murder and the missing necklace. Things looked a little better for Efrem in her own mind, considering the speculations and possible conclusions they'd come up with. At least there was room for doubt but she still wasn't sure how she felt about him. After all, he was found near the scene of the crime and although he seemed like a decent man, his behavior at the shop had unnerved her. When he was frantic he could be capable of anything she supposed.

Then again, what about Mary Ann and her temper? And how desperate was Dirk to win back Kitty? It also bothered her that Irene could be involved, directly or indirectly due to Eddie. The girls had decided that they would speak to her first thing this morning, no matter how much they did not want to do it. They knew she led a wild life, but it was none of their business and usually they didn't want to know the details. However, this instance concerned the store and that made it another matter.

Promptly at 7 a.m., there was a light, but distinct knock on her bedroom door. It was Eleanor, the family maid, who brought her coffee and fresh squeezed orange juice to get her day off right. "Good morning, Miss Daphne. Pleasant night?"

Daphne greeted the housekeeper fondly, as she had been with the family for many years and it felt as if she was one of them. "Not bad, but I've had better," she stretched and yawned as she reached for her light blue cotton lace-trimmed robe that matched her nightie, another one of her favorites from Poppy Cove. It was modest in its coverage, but still fun and a little flirty. "Has the paper come yet?"

"Your father is downstairs reading it as we speak, with your mother. There were quite the headlines today. Your parents were both commenting on that poor young girl. It was on the front page and the society column," Eleanor sighed and tisked as she moved around the room, setting the tray down in the bay window seating area of Daphne's bedroom. "Anything else you need this morning, dear?"

"No, thank you, that's fine. Just tell my parents I'll be down shortly." As Eleanor left, Daphne got up and refreshed herself at the ensuite sink and then sat down to have her coffee and orange juice. She was eager to read the news but on second thought, decided that it could wait. She would rather have a few moments to think about the good things in her life instead. It was another beautiful day with the sun rising up over the gently rolling hillside with just a hint of cool air under the heat of the new day. She took a sip of her juice and smiled to herself. With all that was going on, she forgot that she'd made a date with Daniel for tonight. The more she thought about him, the wider her smile became until her whole face lit up. She always had an active dating life from the age of seventeen when her parents first let her go out on car dates in high school with peers that they approved of.

Most of the young men she'd dated had been from high school or college, coming from the well-established families of Santa Lucia. The majority of them still lived at home on their families' estates, even after graduating, building their own social footing and careers and in many ways had not grown up. They were more like playboys than responsible pillars of the community. As she was now twenty-five years old, she was looking for a more solid man. Recently, she had experienced some new dating situations with one prospective partner being more dangerous than she'd bargained for.

Daniel, like her and the rest of her social set, had grown up in a privileged household. However, he was far more independent, seemed to know who he was and was eager to discover what he wanted in life. His parents, Madeleine and Nicholas Henshaw, ran a profitable business breeding and raising Arabian horses on their ranch near Ojai. His older brother, Victor, was very involved in the family's affairs, as he was poised to take over when their father wanted to retire, but Daniel broke away and was making a path for himself. He still loved horses and wanted to be involved with them, so when the late Constance Stearns-Montgomery, the Santa Lucia socialite and long time client of his family had invited him to be the riding instructor at the new Stearns Academy, he took the opportunity. He moved twenty miles and worlds away to his new position at the school and into a small ranch house at the Academy.

Daphne greatly admired his resolve to start fresh away from a business that would be handed to him if he chose it and understood the feeling of coming into a person's own. For her, she had spent years drifting and unfocused although she did complete her Bachelor of Arts degree at the University of California-Santa Lucia campus, followed by a two-month European tour. Then she returned home to volunteer at charity events and generally socialize, all the while thinking that there must be something more waiting for her to do. She loved shopping, especially for little trinkets, purses and the finer finishing touches to make a girl feel complete. Then one day, just over three years ago she noticed

Margot, a new girl in town around her age sitting and drawing beautifully glamorous dresses in her sketchbook at the Poppy Lane Tearoom. She approached her and the two became fast friends. Within a month, they had started making plans for a business adventure where her shopping savvy was put into great use as an accessories buyer to complement Margot's designs.

Now that she had a feeling of purpose, a career that kept her focused and happy, Daphne's thoughts returned once again to love and romance. Her older brother, William, had been married to Grace for two years now with their first child due in a couple of weeks. He was well established in their father's business and living independently in the carriage house on the estate. It gave her the feeling that it was time to think about settling down. All the casual dates and affairs were becoming a little tiresome. Would Daniel turn out to be the one she would spend the rest of her life with? The thought made her both smile and a little nervous. It gave her a thrill actually if she were honest with herself. She gave her head a little shake, got up from her table and began to get dressed for the day.

She went to her walk-in closet and perused her wardrobe. Now that the news about the Burbanks was hitting the general public, Daphne felt she should wear something subdued from their new fall collection. She picked out a navy wool crepe suit with a slim pencil skirt that had a discreet back slit that gave her plenty of ease to walk and move. It was paired with a short matching boxy jacket. She chose a pewter gray bateau-necked satin blouse to wear underneath. For a little brightness, she put on a new light silver multi-chained necklace that was delicate and flowed like a river in its multiple layers. Once she was dressed, lightly perfumed in Chanel No. 5, powdered and coiffed, she gave herself a quick final glance in the mirror. She felt she was set pretty for the day, her blonde curls all in place, lipstick not too bold but a little too tame for an evening out with her new favorite man. She made sure for her date that night she had a brighter lipstick and smiled to herself as she picked up the small bottle of Tabu, figuring it was time to entice Daniel just that little bit further. Between that and selecting one of the new Poppy Cove evening dresses for tonight when she got to the store, it could lead to a most memorable evening.

Although she was running late, Daphne stopped by the sun porch to greet her parents. She found them there as they were most weekday mornings, her father reading the business news, her mother the society column, commenting back and forth in a comfortable manner. Patricia Huntington-Smythe looked over the top of the *Times* and greeted her daughter. "Good morning, dear. Joining us for breakfast?" Her father Gerald gave an absentminded smile and went back to his page.

"Thank you, no. I have to get going." Behind them, came a commotion from the staircase, into the foyer, around the corner and into the back room. It was Lizzie, her younger sister. She was a senior in high school, pretty in a long-limbed athletic way but a whirlwind of energy which resulted in a ponytail that had ends that stuck out in too many directions, a shirt that had started out pressed and was now wrinkled and one bobby sock up and the other scrunched down in her saddle shoe. Lizzie grabbed a piece of toast from the rack on the table, guzzled down a glass of juice, dribbling on the fresh tablecloth, gave her mother a quick peck on the cheek, briefly acknowledged the rest of her family and flew out the door as fast as she came in, muttering something about early practice before classes.

Patricia absentmindedly touched her cheek and realized there was lipstick on her fingertips. From Lizzie? "Well, will wonders never cease! I think your sister had lipstick on!"

Daphne gave a jolt of surprise. "Lizzie? Really? That would be a first." Their mother had been trying for years to encourage her youngest daughter to become more ladylike, but so far to no avail. She had been more interested in sports, climbing trees and recently salacious detective novels and crime magazines more than beauty and fashion. Daphne smiled, thinking about how her sister may be changing. She noticed Lizzie's behavior was different lately around James Worth, a boy her age who was a family friend and classmate who they often had a Sunday tennis doubles match with at the yacht club. She seemed to be a little softer. Daphne frequently caught her sister watching her in the mirror and mimicking some of her actions, as well as fingering her wardrobe and makeup. Come to think of it, she was getting a little more curious about Daphne's love life too, sometimes asking some rather impertinent questions. "I think she's seeing James in a different light these days."

Patricia gave a little chuckle. "It's about time. They would be a very good match." The older Worth son, Robert was in his early twenties and earmarked to follow his father, Henry, into their family's law practice. James was an amiable teenager and quite likely to do the same. The Worths and the Huntington-Smythes were long standing friends and business associates with the Worth matriarch, Clara, often joining Patricia on charity committees and fundraisers.

Daphne shrugged, somewhat agreeing with her mother. "It's nice to see her take an interest in her appearance and boys. It's a little early to be picking out china patterns though," she chuckled.

Her mother smiled back. "Yes, you're right. I just don't know what we are going to do with her. William's settled down, you've found something that keeps you happy in the meantime, but Lizzie, well, she's all over the place."

"Oh, but she's so young! Girls her age now have so much to choose from, even more than I did. Don't worry—she's a good girl and we'll all be around to help guide her."

"I know but honestly, I do see her with James," her mother confirmed. "I just do."

Daphne quickly scanned the paper in her mother's hands, changing the subject. "I guess Nora's murder made the headlines today?"

"Isn't that something? It's just horrid. That new jeweler seems to be involved," Patricia remarked as she set down the pages.

Daphne gulped and decided to take a seat. She was a little surprised that after all they'd talked about with Loretta, that she had included that in her society column. "Loretta put that in the *Times*?" Even though she wanted to get to work, she decided to take a few minutes to peruse the articles.

"No, dear. That Weathers fellow had it in the main section. Your father has it." For the first time since his daughters had come into the room, Gerald set down his paper. The balding yet distinguished, handsome man got up from the table, gave his wife and daughter pecks on the cheek and made his way to work. Daphne picked up the news section.

The Santa Lucia Times headline read: 'Death of a Beauty Queen.' Michael Weathers had composed a strong story that was sensationalistic, but seemingly accurate. He reported that Nora had been bludgeoned to death in her bed by her own scepter, with the necklace stolen and Efrem Goldberg arrested after being found sleeping and intoxicated in his car just down the street with a necklace in his possession. The story was accompanied with a large photo of the crime scene, heartbreaking in that Nora's lifeless body was clearly depicted with a bare arm flung out from under bloodstained sheets and the scepter on the bedroom floor. At the bottom of the page was a picture of Efrem, which Jake must have taken back stage at the ball and a pageant image of the victim holding the very same scepter. As horrific as it was, Daphne had to admit it was compelling. The reporter had stuck to the facts he'd known at the time with no mention of other possible suspects. She set it down and then picked up the society section where Loretta had tastefully done an in-memoriam style homage to Nora and the rest of the Burbanks that featured pictures of Nora, her mother and other Miss Santa Lucia images in happier times. All in all, it made her sad.

Patricia spoke, bringing her daughter out of her reverie. "Dear, I don't mean to nag, but shouldn't you be on your way? It's getting late. Who's opening the store today?"

"Oh, right! I do have to fly!" She glanced quickly at her watch, realizing that it was almost nine. Poppy Cove was bound to have been opened by Margot, Marjorie or Irene. They all had keys and one, if not all, would be there before her today.

As Daphne got up, her mother asked, "What are your plans tonight? Will you be home for dinner?"

"No, I've got a date with Daniel."

"That's nice. He seems like a good young man. Certainly dances well." Patricia got to know him a little better at the Charity Ball and he left a good impression. "We should have him over for dinner soon. I'll have Eleanor make roast lamb."

"Sounds great. We'll talk about it soon." She made a quick retreat, not only because she was now late, but also because she just didn't feel like she wanted to do that just yet. Daphne felt a little funny as she made her way to her car thinking about it. Most of her past beaus were well known to her family but Daniel was different, being new to Santa Lucia and their whole social set. Somehow, she had this feeling that she wanted to keep him to herself for a while longer. It was new to her and oddly she was enjoying it. She gave her head a little shake and drove away in her convertible.

CHAPTER EIGHT

Margot came in the shop just after nine and found Marjorie getting her team assembled and ready to take on the day's work. If she thought too hard about it all she would get overwhelmed. She thanked God for Marjorie's amazing organizational skills. Having someone so talented and professional at the construction left Margot the freedom to think and play. She was able to let her mind wander into the shapes, silhouettes and colors.

Normally Marjorie's blue eyes sparkled with excited energy, but today the corners seemed a tad world-weary and watery. She appeared fretful with her wavy white/blonde hair looking more wiry than usual as it tried to escape from its updo. "Good morning, Margot. It's a sad business about poor young Nora," she tutted and played with the pencil and notepad in her hands. "To think she was murdered in her own bed, with her parents in the same house! I just don't know what this world is coming to."

Margot put her arm around her friend's shoulder and sighed. She didn't know what to say. When she first arrived in Santa Lucia about three years ago, she felt that she was at home. It was quiet and safe, a good place to start over and make new friends with a clean slate. But now, in the course of a couple of months, two upstanding women of the community were gone. Not only gone, but murdered. She had no idea what their little world was coming to, either. "I know. I don't have any answers for you. Maybe the best thing we can do is carry on with our work."

Marjorie thought for a moment and then asked, "Have you thought about how the news might affect what people would want to wear? I would guess that most of our clientele would be in a somber mood right now."

Margot considered her comments. She knew that for herself this morning she chose a simple black tropical wool shift dress that was very understated and demure. It had a jewel neckline, gently tapering through the bodice that finished below the knee. At first, she chose a bright cherry shirtdress with three-quarter-length French cuffs and a wide sweeping full skirt, but once she saw the front page of the *Times* in the morning with its murder scene, the bright red felt tasteless. She wondered how many of their clientele would feel the same way until the case was solved or until the girl was laid to rest. Mourning clothes might be in demand. She felt somewhat guilty for thinking about business at a time like this, but clothing was a need that Poppy Cove could fill. In their own way, they could help their set in coming to terms with their loss. Also, being practical kept her mind together and from dwelling in grief too much. "Right, you have a point. How is our stock of the navy, gray and black day separates and dresses?"

Marjorie looked at her notebook, turning to her inventory numbers. "The grays have sold well, mainly those pencil skirts. The black trapeze swing coats have moved rapidly, too. The navy shifts are almost all sold out."

"And on the bolts?"

"Plenty of yards left of each and none spoken for with custom orders in those specific fabrics at this point."

"Okay. Let's do this. Keep up with the custom orders for the holiday and evening wear and any others we have, but for this week only, put aside any of the fancier regular stock garments and whip up some day pieces in the more sedate tones. Can our girls get more of those done in such a short time?"

"I think so. We've still got the patterns hung out and they've just recently been working on them, so they should have the routine still in their systems." The two women reflected quietly for a few moments about their new plans. Marjorie had a quizzical look on her face.

Margot stopped scribbling notes and caught her eye. "What is it?"

"Well, now, I don't know if I should say," Marjorie hesitated. Margot waited for her to continue. "It's just that I wonder how much our young ladies at the shop have to do with any of this or what they know."

"Do you mean Irene?"

"Actually, I mean her and Betty as well."

"You mean because of Efrem?"

"Well, yes. The article in the *Times* says he is the main suspect and he is married to Betty's best friend. He was here in the store on Monday, wasn't he?"

Margot answered cautiously. She knew Marjorie was in the back, helping to organize the fashion show returns when Efrem came in, but wasn't sure how much she knew about the situation or the scene he'd caused. "Yes, he was." She was also aware that the girls in the back were big gossips as they worked. She wondered what conclusions they had jumped to. Weathers had discovered that Efrem had been found with the replica necklace after the paper had gone to press and so far that information was not being reported on the radio or television news.

"And Betty was all in a flutter yesterday when he was missing," Marjorie remarked. "So much so that she went home early when her friend Mrs. Goldberg called."

"That's all true, but do you really think that Betty would have anything to do with it?"

Marjorie was quick to reassure Margot of her thoughts. She reached out and patted her arm and emitted a small, relieved laugh. "Oh, no, I don't mean that she was involved in the murder. No, not at all. I just wonder if she may know anything or if she might have overheard something that Mr. Goldberg or even his wife may have said. Or if she'd seen something at the fashion show, before or after, that at the time didn't seem like much but now makes sense."

"Yes, I suppose you're right. I'll speak to her and make sure that she's talked to Tom or one of the other officers if she knows anything. They may have already contacted her and Dwight for that matter."

Margot considered her seamstress's personal character. Marjorie was the soul of discretion and Margot decided to tell her about what they'd found out last night from Michael Weathers regarding Efrem's scratched arms and being found with the replica.

Marjorie gave some thought to the information. "This case is getting more and more curious by the moment. Now we don't know what he said, did or said he did, but it's odd that he would have scratched up arms *and* the replica. Why would that be? If he was found with the real necklace and scratched arms, it would be very clear that he'd been in a struggle with Nora or the window to get the necklace. Being found with what he had on him leaves room for doubt, but he was up to something that's certain." Marjorie straightened up her papers with a firm shuffle. "As for Irene, she's a different story altogether."

"Meaning?"

"Meaning that I wouldn't be surprised to find out that her Eddie had something to do with it. And I doubt very much that Irene would turn away stolen jewels if they were offered to her!"

"Are you suggesting that Eddie and Efrem were in cahoots and Irene was the reason behind it?" The idea boggled Margot's mind. She thought about Dirk, too and his evening out with Efrem, as well as the comments he made at the show about his ex-wife. Were they all involved?

Marjorie gave a nonchalant shrug. "I don't know anything for certain, just that I'd have a chat with Irene soon and find out for yourself what she's been up to." She patted Margot on the arm and gave her a reassuring smile, as she realized how seriously her employer was taking in her words. "Oh, don't listen to me, I'm just speculating. Chances are she wouldn't do anything so low, but you'll feel better once you've cleared the air with her."

While the older woman made her way to the sewing room, Margot continued fretting, which was not how she usually liked to handle things. When there was a thought to question someone's actions or behavior, she preferred to stick to the facts and not let her emotions run away with her. Fortunately, she did not have to wait long as Irene came sauntering in. She wanted to wait for Daphne to arrive but the time to talk seemed right. The store was quiet and her mind was set for the task.

"Good morning, Irene. How was your evening last night?"

Irene gave a little shrug and tilt of her head. "It was a nothing night."

Margot could only imagine what she meant by that. "Eddie didn't call?"

"Oh, him? No. I stayed in, washed my hair, did my nails." She perused the appointment book as she sipped her coffee, unaware or not caring that her employer was attempting to have a discussion with her.

Margot looked down at Irene's nails that were a tangerine orange matching her tight-fitting surplice wrap blouse, tied at the waist with a wide sash. She had paired it with the gray pencil skirt she'd worn yesterday, which was the only subtle thing about her. Margot was considering how to bring up Marjorie's theory when Daphne came in.

She greeted them both as she took in their appearances. She noted that Margot had shared her own feelings about the expectations of Santa Lucians' mourning response, whereas Irene, in her bright, vibrant tones, had paid it no heed. She caught the drift of her business partner, sensed her anxiety and assumed correctly that she was ready to interrogate their manager. The two had a quick, quiet word and Margot left briefly to ask Marjorie to cover the store. When she reappeared, Margot suggested to Irene that they all should go upstairs. Once they were behind the closed office door, Daphne decided to jump right in and asked, "Irene, what do you know about what happened to Nora and the necklace?"

Margot sucked in her breath in reaction to the directness of her friend. Irene sat still in her chair and looked Daphne squarely in the eye. "What exactly are you asking me?"

Daphne laid her thoughts out on the table. "The night of Nora's murder, you were there at Bud's and saw Dirk and Efrem talking. You were also here when Efrem was saying that the real necklace was at Nora's. Eddie made some noises about wanting the necklace to win you over at the fashion show. Efrem was found with the replica by the police, and there's doubt as to whether or not he's involved in the murder—and now the real necklace is missing."

Irene was silent for a moment, staring down her employers. "So you are accusing me of both theft and murder," Irene icily stated.

Margot stepped in and did her best to mediate. She needed to smooth over the waters, but all the same wanted answers. "No, I don't think that's what Daphne's saying. We just want to know if you know anything about it. If you overheard Dirk or Efrem say anything that at the time seemed like nothing or if Eddie and his friends had any dealings with the situation, that's all."

Irene sat coolly for what seemed like an eternity. "No. Look, I told you all I knew about from Bud's on Monday night. As for Eddie, I'm not his keeper. All I heard from him yesterday was that he was lying low. Far as I'm concerned, that could mean anything. I don't care that much about him or his hobbies, either." She sat there rigidly, arms folded and defiant. In the silence, she finally moved, slouched and softened slightly. "Listen, I'm sorry that Nora's been killed, but I had nothing to do with it. I may be looking for a little excitement in this town, but I know when bad is bad and it crosses a line. I don't do that and honestly, I'm angry that you two would think so little of me."

Irene's admission of vulnerability to their poor impression of her rapidly turned the situation. Margot and Daphne felt guilty about their jumping on her like this and wanted to reassure the person who they trusted their business to that they still did. Daphne replied in a rush of words, "Sorry, Irene. It's just that this is so upsetting and another murder so close to home again has us all questioning everything. We know that deep down, you're trustworthy and have a smart sense of life."

Irene replied. "I've done a lot of things in my life. Some I'm proud of, some of it's none of your business.

But anything I've done has been what I've chosen to do, and not at the expense of anyone else's life."

"Right," Margot confirmed. Irene was starting to get fidgety and although she wanted to reach out and give the girl a reassuring hug, she knew that was not Irene's style. The best thing would be to leave her alone and give her space to work out her feelings. "We know you're okay. Just if anything comes to mind that you remember later, give Tom a call."

Irene gave a nod and looked at them both mutely, obviously wanting to leave the room. Margot motioned a dismissal and let her go back downstairs. She shut the door behind her on the way down.

"Wow, glad that's over." Daphne slumped in her chair. "That was so awkward. It's a good thing we handled that together."

Margot sighed and nodded in agreement. "I felt so bad that we put her on the spot like that, but it's good to know that she wasn't involved."

"Did you really think she would be?"

"No, not really. Not directly, anyway. She does know some shady characters, though. It was odd that she was there at Bud's and could possibly have overheard something."

"Honestly, knowing Irene, it isn't surprising she'd be at a dive bar. The truly odd thing is Efrem being there."

Margot paused a moment to rifle through a swatch catalogue on her desk. "Wonder if they've pieced together anything more of his night yet."

Daphne eagerly perked up. "Can you call Tom?"

Margot looked at her, suppressing a grin. "I really shouldn't. After all, none of this is any of our business is it, really?"

"Well." Behind Daphne's curls, her brain was working out her own unique brand of logic. "Efrem did get us involved with it all. He did come here first and we were going to do the switch at the store. And, we did interrogate Irene for the police, saving them a step, right? You could always share that with him and suggest that he shares a little with you, being that it's an exchange of information, of course."

Margot had to admit she wanted to know what was going on with Efrem. None of it made sense and she always felt better when things were neat and tidy. And Tom did need to know that they had talked with Irene and what she'd said. That way he could make an educated decision on whether or not she needed to be brought in and questioned about what she might have casually overheard. It made sense to her and she picked up the phone. "Yes, he should know what we did."

"And if the subject of lunch does come up, I'll be happy to cover for you for as long as it takes for you to find out what Efrem did," Daphne concluded. "Your policeman boyfriend should have some answers by then."

Margot laughed and called Tom. She left a message for him with Penny, as he was busy, no doubt questioning Efrem, Margot imagined. She expressed to her friend and client, the switchboard operator, that she was genuinely concerned about Tom's well being and urged her to make sure that she gave her man the message that he needed to eat. Also, to tell him that Margot would be happy to join him for lunch whenever he could take a break.

Even though the case was on Margot's mind, she had to admit that having an excuse to see Tom in the middle of the day would make it brighter. She had never felt so safe in a man's presence before. She grew up in a stable home, wanting for nothing and had known other men in her life but Tom was strong, solid and sure. He had never rushed her in their relationship, although she knew that after all this time that it would make perfect sense that he may be yearning for a more permanent situation with her. For the first time, the thought of such a situation made her happy, not reticent.

Margot looked over at Daphne. "So, what are your plans with Daniel? When's your next date?"

"Tonight. Which reminds me—help me pick out a dress from downstairs."

"Sure. Where are you going?"

"I don't know. He says he wants to surprise me. Given that we had such a great time dancing at the ball, I'm thinking that I'd better pick out something that I can dance in, and maybe a halter style or something with straps," Daphne remarked.

Having their uncomfortable episode with Irene behind them, the girls bounded downstairs to play in the party dresses. By the time they were on the sales floor, Irene was busy helping a customer with purchases and seemed back to her usual demeanor. Seeing that, Margot and Daphne were happy to give into a great excuse to put the somber feelings aside and have a little fun. As they flipped through the racks, Daphne zeroed in on one of her favorite new gowns of the season. It was a full-length black silk taffeta and organza creation, with a halter v-neck and shirred through the breast line, snuggly fitting under the bust to the waist, then with a sweeping full skirt dramatically down to the floor. It was a stunner and sure to make Daniel's jaw drop when he saw her. "Oh, this is it! Between this and Tabu, he won't stand a chance!" she exclaimed as she held it up against herself.

Margot smiled and slightly wrinkled her nose and forehead. It was definitely a dress for dancing, romancing and entrancing, and would certainly suit Daphne, but it was also very formal. *Too formal*, she thought, *for a Wednesday evening date without set plans.* She pulled another dress off the rack and handed it to Daphne. "What about this one?"

Daphne hung the black dress back up and had a look at Margot's offering. It was a similar version of the black one, but in white with large black polka-dotted organza over the white taffeta. The full skirt was tea length rather than all the way to the floor. As she placed it against herself, she remarked, "Say, I like this one, too." She gave a little swish and sway to see how it moved. "You're right; this one's better for a Wednesday night date. Plus, it shows off my legs!" Daphne's ankles and calves were very daintily well defined from all of her athletic pursuits. "I've got those new black patent pumps from the fashion show that would be just darling with it."

"Absolutely! Go ahead and take it upstairs. I'll write it up in the sales ledger," Margot agreed. Whenever the girls took something home for their own personal use, they kept track of it to be run through the books by their accountant.

As Daphne did just that, there was a strong, odd odor wafting from the shop's open front door. Margot looked over to see the Baroness Eva von Eissen, dressed severely in black Victorian lace, with an old-fashioned corseted waistline, full skirt, long sleeves and high-necked collar. The scent, Margot realized, was mothballs. "Baroness, welcome to Poppy Cove. How can we be of service?" She wasn't sure exactly how to greet a woman of such a title and gave a small bow that could be interpreted as a curtsey or just a reach to straighten out a rack.

The older, staid woman stared at her for a moment, sizing her up. Eventually, she replied in a thick, eastern European accent, "I require a wardrobe suitable to the climate, now that I have chosen to permanently reside in Santa Lucia."

Margot could not agree more but played it cool. It was apparent by the Baroness's demeanor that she was used to commanding what she wanted, rather than open to listening to suggestions from someone who she considered to be in a subservient position. "Certainly. Would you like to make an appointment?"

"No. I would like to discuss the matter now. The garments I have for public appearances were inherited down through my family and are apparently deemed inappropriate for what is considered elite society in this town."

By this time, Daphne had bounded back downstairs and was startled to see their newest client. She recovered from her surprised expression by noticing Baroness von Eissen's jet-black beads that she was toying with as she talked with Margot. "Baroness, it's a pleasure to have you in our store. Your necklace is lovely. Is it a family heirloom?"

The Baroness slowly turned to face the new person in the conversation. "Yes. They were passed down from my husband's mother and her mother before her." She swept her eyes around the room, scanning the garments. "Most of your wares are quite youthful and bright. I am still in mourning for my late husband, Baron Vladimir. I'll need apparel in darker tones and lines to suit my age."

Daphne attempted friendship. "Oh, I'm sorry to hear of your loss. How long has your husband been gone?" There had been rumors surrounding the death of the Baron. From what was the talk of the town, the Baroness had moved to Santa Lucia from somewhere in Eastern Europe about three or four months ago, already widowed. There were apparently also a couple of sons but no one had seen them all together.

Margot gave a critical look to gauge the woman's appearance. The dusty and severe clothes made her appear older than she probably was. The overbearing hat hid a lightly-lined face, not too saggy, and layers of clothing covered a figure that was most likely curvy and full, buxom but still retaining an hourglass shape. The designer felt that she certainly could help the Baroness if the matron would allow. "Let me just check my appointment book."

The Baroness's cold blue eyes narrowed. "You should know if you have any pressing matters. It's only the start of the day. It can't be that hard to keep track of your orders," she sniffed.

Margot understood that she was trying to undermine her and did not fall for the intimidation. She took her time to peruse the book and compose herself. She didn't have any appointments scheduled until two o'clock. "I can make some time for you now. Why don't you take a closer look at what we have while I get my materials and ask Marjorie to join us?"

As the Baroness walked around the garments, she fingered one, then another, paused at some and sniffed at others. Nancy Lewis entered the store and met up with the woman from the other end of the new fall suits. "Oh, Baroness, it's so wonderful to see you again."

The Baroness looked Nancy up and down and finished with a blank expression. Nancy continued: "We met at the fashion show on Saturday night. You must remember!" The slim woman with her Baroness did not take. "I'm Nancy Lewis. My husband Andrew is in charge of the First Bank of Santa Lucia." She paused. "Well, no matter. I'm on many of the social committees around town and would consider it an honor to introduce you to all the right people, Eva."

"My title is Baroness von Eissen. You will refer to me by my title." The Baroness continued around the store, passing her by, indifferent to her new acquaintance.

"Well, of all the nerve!" exclaimed a miffed Nancy, but she was undaunted. The redheaded, birdlike woman dashed around the next rack of career day dresses to catch up with the doyenne. Ever the social climber, Nancy felt that the new resident royalty was someone she needed to befriend. "I believe we may have a family member in common," she blurted out less elegantly than she wanted to, stepping awkwardly in front of the Baroness.

From a distance at the sales counter, Daphne and Irene were watching. If things got out of hand, Daphne would step in and diffuse the situation, but for the moment, it was quite amusing. The Baroness actually seemed to be enjoying the chase in her own remote way. Both Daphne and Irene knew what was coming; they'd seen Nancy pull this one before. No one believed her, but most found it great sport to watch her try to impress others with her made up family history.

The Baroness gave no response except for an icy stare and continued to make her way through the garments. Nancy was not discouraged. "I'm related to Danish royalty!"

"I see." The Baroness stopped and let her continue.

Nancy beamed as if she had an 'in.' "Yes. Princess Bettina. Third cousin, I believe, on my mother's side, once removed."

The Baroness considered her comment. "Did you say Bettina?"

Eagerly Nancy confirmed, "Yes!"

"I know Princesses Irene, Katherine and Marina intimately. I know of no Bettina. What side of the family is she?"

Nancy was flummoxed. Whenever she'd mentioned that she was related to Danish royalty, no one had ever questioned her further. "Oh, um," she stammered, "Rosenborg."

"No. No Bettina in the Rosenborg line."

"Well, uh, I could be pronouncing it wrong. I believe the accent may be on the last or middle syllable."

The Baroness continued to glare her down. "You must be mistaken. I understand there is a dairy company, Rosenborg, not related, that produces blue cheese; they have a milk maiden on their label. She must be your Bettina." She turned away from Nancy. "I will sit over here and wait for Miss Williams to attend to me."

Daphne and Irene could barely contain themselves as they watched the older woman move to the lounge area, but they remained in polite composure for Nancy's sake. She was a good customer and to acknowledge her humiliation would be the height of bad taste. Fortunately, just then, Margot had returned with Marjorie in tow.

They settled down for their consultation. Daphne, well in control of her faculties, went to Nancy. "What can we help you with today, Mrs. Lewis?" Although they usually called her by her first name, formality seemed to be the best way to help Nancy regain her dignity.

Nancy fussed at a blouse on a nearby hanger. "That's fine, nothing today. I'll...I'll come back. Later, or tomorrow." She barely met Daphne's eye as she scurried out the door. Daphne had to admit she felt a little twinge of sadness for Nancy's humiliation. Nancy Lewis had done and said many things that were careless and arrogant in her forty years, but she came from a family that had had its share of tragedy and heartache. Andrew, her banker husband, was almost old enough to be her father, but doted on her and their marriage gave Nancy social standing, which she frequently abused.

For all of Nancy's gaucheness, there was a sense of pride that one could not help but feel when they knew how little Nancy Harrison had had to struggle to arrive on the top rung of the Santa Lucia social ladder.

Meanwhile, the unexpected appointment with the Baroness was proving to be quite the challenge for Margot. She did not want to be measured, not today. Any colors Margot suggested, were rejected—the gray wools and flannels had too much color, the white silks and shirtings had too much glare, the ivories and creams too yellow, the blacks were the wrong shades of black. Any other colors were dismissed without even a cursory glance. The styles Margot suggested, although modest yet modern, up to date and flattering to what she could only guess of the baroness's shape were frowned upon and considered too revealing for her tastes. It was appearing to be a fruitless effort.

Nevertheless, the Baroness suggested, "Miss Williams, I will give you another chance. I will return for an appointment next week. I suggest you use that time to confer with your seamstress and consider the needs of someone of my stature."

Margot wasn't sure how she felt about continuing the relationship with this client. She certainly wasn't short of orders and didn't know if she could ever make this woman happy. She gave a quick glance at Marjorie who gave a non-committal shrug. *Why not?* she thought. *One more appointment and if nothing appeals to her, we won't pursue it further.*

"Fine," Margot stated. "Come with me to the counter and we'll set up an appointment. In the meantime, I'll consult some of my European fashion magazines and come up with some sketches that will, hopefully, please you." Marjorie went back to the sewing room while the pair went to settle on a date. Daphne and Irene dispersed, not wanting to deal with the woman. As they settled the appointment, the Baroness glanced at the newspaper lying on the counter. She gave a look of disapproval.

Margot was trying to read her expression. "Terrible tragedy about Nora Burbank, isn't it? It's such a shock, but, rest assured, things like this don't usually happen around here."

"There's a rumor that a necklace is missing. The one from the fashion show," stated the Baroness.

The Santa Lucia Times had not reported that information yet, nor had it been on the radio this morning. News did travel fast, but Margot didn't take the Baroness as being part of gossip circles or coffee klatches. "Yes, I've heard that, too. May I ask how you came to hear that information? From what I understand, it isn't public knowledge yet."

"I am very well connected, no matter where I go. I have ways to find answers." She was becoming more cryptic and mysterious with every word she spoke. "I desired the necklace. Now that it is missing, I want it even more. It gives it provenance and intrigue. That jeweler was found with a paste copy, I understand."

"Yes," Margot confirmed. There was no need to hide what she already knew, as the Baroness seemed to know more about it than they did.

"The girl was killed for the real diamonds. They must be found. Otherwise, her death was completely useless." The statement was flat.

Margot felt like the ground had dropped beneath her. Rarely was the unflappable designer ruffled. Angrily she replied, "There is never a need for murder." Irene and Daphne stopped what they were doing, looked at each other, forgetting any trace of coldness, distrust and animosity from earlier in the morning between them. They came over and stood behind the Baroness and watched Margot, letting her command the scene, but ready to jump in if necessary.

The Baroness pursed her lips, sensing she'd gone too far. "Yes, of course. Perhaps in my broken English, what I say comes out wrong. It is always a tragedy when a life is taken."

Margot felt the tension in the room ease a bit and decided to give the woman the benefit of the doubt. She flipped through the appointment book and brought the discussion back to the matter at hand. "How would Tuesday the 8th at 2 p.m. suit you?"

"Fine. I look forward to seeing your ideas." The Baroness visibly softened as she replied. "I must consider my situation and surroundings. The American life, especially here in Santa Lucia, is much more libertine and heedless. I suppose I must compromise some of my ways to take my place in this society."

Daphne and Irene looked at each other behind her back, agog at her language. They recovered their composed professional expressions just before Margot thought she would lose hers. "I'm sure we can come up with a wardrobe that will be both fashionable and suitable to your sensibilities." *At least,* Margot thought, *I'll give it a go.*

"Wow," exclaimed Irene after the royal departure. Her simple comment summed up the thoughts of the whole group.

Daphne remarked, "So do you think you can come up with something she'll like?"

"Honestly, I don't know." It was rare that Margot could not come up with a custom design to please a client. She hated the idea of turning business away in general but she had her doubts that this woman could be pleased and anticipated that she might turn out to be more headache than profit.

"What about that remark about Nora? Who would think those things, let alone say them?" Daphne continued to ramble while she fussed with the hangers. "You don't think she had something to do with the murder, do you?"

Margot was distracted, with her head in her sketchbook, already dreaming of ways to conquer this new design challenge. She considered the Baroness's ample figure and her need for modesty. She'd start with a fitted jacket with a peplum, puffed sleeves and generous shoulder pads that would balance out her shape and would be reflective of the Victorian style she was accustomed to. She could pair it with a slimming skirt, ending just above the ankle with a comfortable back pleat for ease of walking. Dark gray flannel would be a suitable choice for her. At least it was a starting point. Margot felt a glimmer of promise when she realized that a feminine modern version of the Baroness's antiquated wardrobe could be the answer she was looking for. She looked up and saw Daphne blankly staring at her. "Sorry, what were you saying?"

Daphne harrumphed exasperatedly, rolling her eyes. "The Baroness and the murder. She was so cold about it. I'm wondering if she had something to do with it."

"You've got to be kidding. Could you really imagine her climbing through a bedroom window in one of her corseted gowns?" Margot laughed out loud at the thought.

"No, not her directly, but what if she paid someone to steal the necklace and kill Nora?"

Margot wasn't seeing Daphne's trail of logic. "No one knew that Nora had the real necklace, other than Efrem and us."

Daphne shrugged. "Well, who really knows who knew what? Obviously, someone did know that she had the real necklace and that someone may be in addition to Efrem."

Margot considered her remarks and shook her head. "I think I have a direction for the Baroness's wardrobe. I'm going upstairs for awhile."

CHAPTER NINE

As Margot left, Daphne continued to stew about it. Fortunately, the store became busy and only Irene and she were left to tend to the customers. Even though there had not been a date set for Nora's funeral, every young college girl seemed to be coming in for the occasion. As Marjorie and Margot had predicted, they were rapidly selling out of navy, dark gray and black garments, but it was disheartening to see all the pretty young girls with red eyes and snuffly noses. Daphne realized that both Mary Ann Rutherford and Caroline Parker, the Santa Lucia Princesses, were in the store. Before long, there was a nasty exchange brewing.

"Well, I hope you're happy now. You've got what you've wanted," spat out Caroline. The snappish tone was out of character for the demure Miss Parker. Daphne was surprised while Irene raised an eyebrow and smirked at the remark.

"Whatever do you mean by that?" Mary Ann replied through gritted teeth while focusing her slitted eyes on her fellow princess.

"You hated it that Nora won the title over you! You even demanded a recount and you still lost. Well, it looks like you won after all."

"What are you insinuating, Caroline? Are you seriously implying that I would commit murder for a cheap tin crown?"

"You certainly gave that impression ever since Nora won. You two were constantly fighting about everything—the pageant protocols, the necklace,

Nora's boyfriend Ralph. You even managed to split them up!"

Mary Ann blithely waived the navy shift dress she had in her hand in the general direction of her sparring partner. "Who, Ralph? Listen, it's not my fault he liked me more than her."

Daphne continued to listen intently and considered breaking it up, but had to admit she was enthralled with all the information she was learning about the rumors surrounding Nora. She wouldn't step in unless more customers came in or they looked like they would inflict damage on the store. Ralph must have been the young man Nora had been seeing during the summer. Or had still been seeing after Nora began to use a lock on her bedroom door? If she was seeing a boy on the sly that her parents didn't like, that would certainly explain to Daphne why she'd want to keep secrets. Maybe she wasn't as innocent as they had all thought? Had Ralph been the murderer and thief who'd climbed through her window Monday night?

Caroline took one step bolder in her accusations. "Where are you hiding the necklace, Mary Ann? Who has it, you or Ralph?" She grabbed the wooden hanger from Mary Ann's grasp and, in her anger, snapped it in two.

"Girls! That's no way to behave." Daphne stepped over and took the dress and hanger from Caroline's trembling hands.

"Yes, I would agree. Break it up or I'll be forced to." All eyes turned to the front door in response to the deep male voice of Detective Tom Malone as he entered the store, accompanied by Detective Riley and Officer Jenkins.

Daphne smiled in relief when she saw him. "Oh, am I pleased to see you! I'll go get Margot; it must be lunchtime by now." Not only had Tom's timing been perfect to keep Poppy Cove from sustaining damage, but also their plan of getting more information about Efrem might now fall into place.

Tom cleared his throat before he spoke. "I'm not here for a lunch date. We'll need to speak with her as well," Tom stated flatly. As Santa Lucia's lead detective and being six foot two in stature, Tom's very presence commanded order. It was also clear that while being immaculately dressed in his natty suit and followed by an additional plain-clothed partner and uniformed officer, he was there on official police business. His demeanor became very formal. "We understand that certain members of this store's staff were present on the night of Saturday, September 28th at the Santa Lucia Yacht Club when the alleged exchange of necklaces took place."

From behind Tom's right shoulder, Riley flipped open a small spiral-bound notebook and requested, "We need to speak with Miss Abigail Browning, Mrs. Marjorie Cummings, Miss Daphne Huntington-Smythe, Miss Irene Swanson, Miss Margot Williams and Mrs. Elizabeth Young."

"Being that they are all Poppy Cove staff," Tom acknowledged, "we request the use of one of your private offices to interview the individuals here. Otherwise, we'll have to make arrangements to interview everyone at the station. If we have your permission, it would save the department valuable time and it may help to solve the crimes sooner."

"Crimes?" Daphne questioned.

Riley responded. "Yes. The murder of Miss Nora Burbank and the theft of a diamond necklace."

Daphne sparked. "Would that be the real or replica piece?"

Riley glanced at Tom whose jaw minutely tightened. Riley said nothing.

"So the murder and the theft are being treated as separate crimes?" Daphne continued.

"Not at liberty to say," Tom remarked, abruptly ending any further curious pursuit.

"Well," Daphne replied. "Margot's just upstairs, so I'll go get her. Marjorie and Irene are working today but both Betty and Abigail have the day off. Do you need me to call them in?"

"No, that's not necessary. We'll make arrangements to speak with them later. Where can we conduct the interviews?"

"Please use the lunchroom just behind the wall here." Daphne showed the direction to them, indicating the small room behind the sales desk. Tom gave a nod to his co-workers and they proceeded. Daphne gave a fleeting glance to the two princesses and grasped Tom's arm. Discreetly, she said, "I need to speak with you first."

He nodded and made a gesture for her to accompany him to the makeshift interrogation room. They sat down at the chrome and Formica table and she briefed him on the exchange that she'd just witnessed between Mary Ann and Caroline. He made notes of what she shared with him. Tom sent Riley out to the sales floor to request that the two girls remain in the store until the police had a chance to speak with them as they were on the contact list as well for that night and to get the details on what just happened a few minutes ago. The officer asked Irene to keep the girls apart and make sure they did not speak to one another. Both sat in the salon area, silently staring daggers at one another.

After Tom had interviewed Daphne, she came out and went directly upstairs to get Margot, who then went immediately into the lunchroom to be questioned. As soon as she went in, Tom came out and traded places with the officer on the sales floor while Jenkins and

Riley questioned his girlfriend. "Conflict of interest," he stated for anyone in the room who might be interested that his relationship with the shop owner could affect the case.

Margot's time in the hot seat was very brief, as it was for Marjorie as well. However, Irene's interrogation seemed to go on forever. The sewing room girls, who were used to using the lunchroom at noon sharp, were beginning to get peckish and impatient. Margot and Daphne decided to dip into the cash box and treat the girls to lunch at the Poppy Lane Tearoom just across the way. None of them were present at the fashion show on Saturday night and wouldn't be interviewed by the police.

In the meantime, Margot had noticed the two sulking princesses sitting in the lounge chairs. She walked over to Daphne who was arranging new Julia MacKay evening clutch purses. "What went on here? Did I miss something?"

"I'll say," she whispered to her friend. "I'll tell you later. It was a doozy!"

After Irene came out of her interrogation, she didn't meet anyone's eyes, went directly to the sales desk and began absentmindedly scanning through the appointment book. As she turned the pages, Margot noticed that Irene's hand was shaking, she was very quiet and visibly pale. Margot gently nudged Daphne's elbow and cocked her head in the direction of their manager. Daphne discreetly glanced and gave her partner a quizzical look. Both of them were dying to know what had been said or implied to rattle the ice princess, but knew they wouldn't get anything out of her unless she wanted to talk.

After the police finished the staff questioning, they interviewed Mary Ann and Caroline separately. Each girl came out and sat back down, waiting for further instruction from the police officers. Tom and Riley stayed in the back room, conferring on their findings. Margot and Daphne couldn't help themselves from wanting to hover around the lunchroom door. Finally it opened and the girls busied themselves at a nearby clothes rack. The officers were ready to leave. Tom announced that they were all free to go but must remain in the area if further questioning was needed. Mary Ann and Caroline, who'd been very well behaved under police surveillance, both got up immediately, sniping and bickering all the way, elbowing each other through the front door with Mary Ann in the lead, shoving Caroline back behind her. Riley and Jenkins even smirked at their unladylike behavior but made no movement to follow after them to break up a potential fresh outburst. Some catfights were best left to deflate on their own steam.

It was also clear that Tom was in full policeman mode and not available for the lunch Margot had planned. Being that it was close to 2 p.m. when her custom appointment was due to arrive, she wasn't either. She did have a couple of minutes to see him alone or get a quick bite across the street, but not time for both.

"Well, I'm famished. I'm going to get a sandwich from the Tearoom. Want anything?" Daphne asked.

"You read my mind. A muffin, thanks. Whatever Lana picks. That gives me a chance to talk to Tom for a bit."

"Ooh, tell me what you find out!" Daphne grabbed her purse from under the counter and left.

Margot shook her head gently with a soft laugh. She too was curious about the case but truthfully when he was so busy with situations such as this, all she wanted to do was to have whatever time she could to just be with him. She felt a strong sense of nurturing towards him, to look after her man. Not that she was ready for marriage, not by a long shot. At least she didn't think so. How could she? Poppy Cove still needed her full attention. She gave her head another nod to clear her thoughts and smiled in Tom's direction. He was talking to his co-workers as she walked over to him. His head turned as he heard the click of her heels and gave her a warm smile.

She addressed the group. "Gentlemen, can you spare your detective for a minute?" They all knew her well, as Santa Lucia was still a small town in many ways. Jenkins gave a relaxed gesture and Tom stepped forward to Margot. She led him back to the lunchroom, but left the door open.

He perched himself on the edge of the table and she walked into his arms, giving him a quick peck on the cheek and fussing with his hair, brushing it back with her fingers while he held her in his arms.

"Oh, dear, I was so hoping you'd have time for lunch today. Now, *I* don't even have the time," she sighed. "I called the station and left a message for you. Did you get it?"

"No, sorry, Mar. This case has me all tied up." Although he was making a concerted effort, she could see his mind was a million miles away.

"Anything you want to talk about, darling?" She had to admit to herself that, of course, she cared about him, the man in her life, but if he wanted to tell her anything, wasn't it her duty as his lover to listen, help share his woes? And if she learned anything in the process about the case, well that's the way it is.

Tom relaxed a little more, opened his mouth and was just about to speak. He stopped himself with a playful grin, tapping his fingertip to her nose. "No. You're too close to the situation. You know too many people involved and I don't want you in any further than necessary." He didn't let go of her but sat up a little straighter.

Margot tilted her head coquettishly. She knew she was shamelessly flirting and couldn't tell herself if it was purely for affection or curiosity. She wasn't even sure she cared which it was anymore. "Oh, Tom, I just thought it might help to talk about it."

He laughed. "Now, you don't think I'm buying that one, do you?" Tom became a little more serious. "We've talked about this. You are to stay out of my business and I'll stay out yours. Remember what happened last time?"

"Yes. We helped you catch a killer."

"And one of you got put in harm's way. I mean it, Margot."

Margot messed up his hair, breaking him out of his stern manner. "That's better. Honestly, it's just that I'm concerned about Betty. She's really upset. She can't believe that Efrem's involved."

Tom said nothing. She tried another tack. "I have trouble believing it, too. Is he?"

"Come on," he gently goaded. "You know I can't say anything."

"Well, can you at least tell me if it's true that he had the replica necklace on him?"

"Daphne asked that very same thing earlier. Now how on earth did you two hear about that?"

She shrugged. Telling him it was Loretta would tick him off and possibly get her into trouble. "It's just something that's being said."

"I cannot confirm or deny. No comment. I won't say it again." His jaw was firm but his grip was still relaxed.

"Okay," she said as he smiled again and leaned in for another kiss, but this one was long and lingering.

The only thing that stopped them was the sound of snickering from the doorway as the workroom staff was passing by, stopping to watch and comment on the lovebirds. They were a gossipy bunch, as it helped them work through their day. Marjorie took up the rear and moved them along.

"Margot, it's almost two. Are you all set for Mrs. Stinson?" Marjorie was ready with her notebook, measuring tape and a book of swatches for a fresh consultation with the Mayor's wife. Nancy needed a new day suit for a round of Chamber of Commerce meetings.

The mood was definitely broken up for good when Daphne came bustling in with sandwiches and coffee. "Mar, time for a quick bite. Tom, time for you to go!" She gave him a quick wink but she meant it. The police weren't the only ones with busy days.

Margot flashed her a look, not entirely happy for the interruption. As they were parting, she tried to set up a dinner date for that night. He reluctantly declined, hoping they would be able to spend some time the next evening.

CHAPTER TEN

The rest of the day passed by quickly. The Mayor's wife ordered a rather subdued navy suit, catching the overall spirit of the town's mood. In addition, the girls could not get a word out of Irene. She did her job, was efficient with the customers, but as soon as the day was over, she was out like a shot without a word or nod goodbye. It was out of character for her not to have made a wisecrack or sly remark about at least one person all afternoon.

However, throughout the rest of the day, Daphne's head turned to romance and curiosity wondering what Dan had up his sleeve. *It must involve dancing,* she thought. *After how delightful that night was, it has to.* She gave an audible sigh that left a smile on her face. At closing, she ran upstairs, grabbed her makeup bag and her beautiful new gown. She stepped into the dressing room to get ready.

Daphne took her time primping and preening but when she floated out, she was a vision. The lipstick was just that shade of alluring red, blonde curls just so, her shoulders a perfect toned and bronze late summer shade, all set off by the luminous glow of her white dress. Margot, who'd been busy closing and locking up the shop, couldn't help but admire her friend and the scent wafting through the room in her wake. "Oh, my, time for Tabu!"

Daphne laughed. "Let's just say some things may not be forbidden to him anymore," referring to the powers of the perfume. It was said in such a tone that made Margot's eyebrows rise and Daphne blush. They both giggled.

Margot patted her friend's arm. "Have a great time, Daff. Just don't do anything that I wouldn't do!"

Daphne winked. "You've been going with Tom for a couple of years now. Is there anything left?"

Margot clucked and chided her friend, changing the subject. "Where are you meeting Daniel?"

"Up at his house. He says he has a whole surprise planned." She gently tied a white chiffon headscarf over her perfectly coiffed hair and continued to beam as she glanced at her diamond watch. "Oh, I've got to fly!"

After Daphne left, Margot decided to stay late. With Tom being busy as well and so much to do at the shop, she was hoping to get the new orders straightened out and maybe spend a little time playing with the swatches for the spring collection. She enjoyed her quiet time upstairs, sitting up in the office looking out of the big arched window overlooking the fountain, with jazz low on the radio and drawing away through the evening. It's when her best ideas came. Years ago, when they were in the early days of Poppy Cove, she lived upstairs, very cozy and happy, lost in planning a new future. As things became steadier and busier with the business, she found her cute little bungalow two blocks away and adopted Mr. Cuddles, a stray kitten that showed up on her doorstep. Although she felt very much at home in her cottage, the office always gave her a welcome feeling.

Daphne drummed her fingertips along with Paul Anka's *Diana* playing on the radio. She pulled into the Academy parking lot and saw Daniel leaning on his Plymouth Fury, a sharp little two-door in its shimmery sand dune white. He smiled and gave her a little wave as she pulled into a spot near him. She gave him a quizzical look, surprised at his attire. He looked handsome, of course, with his sandy blonde hair, hazel eyes and tall athletic build, but he was wearing his red checked short-sleeved shirt and black chinos. She removed her headscarf and gave herself a once over in her rearview mirror, dabbing with her lipstick. She must have been early and felt a little awkward about her eagerness.

"Daniel!" She greeted him as he opened her car door and gave her a peck on the lips. "Am I early? Do you need to go home and change?"

He was visibly wowed with her appearance and noticed the lingering, seductive scent around her. "No, I'm all set. You, by the way, look more beautiful every time I see you."

She heard his compliment and was flattered but a little confused. "Well, if you're dressed and ready to go, where are you taking me? Am I overdressed?" Daphne was usually ready for anything but clearly felt out of place.

"I told you—I have it all worked out." As he escorted her into his car, he noticed her anxiety and gave her another warm smile to reassure her of his intentions. "Don't worry, you look lovely. I'll be very proud to have you on my arm tonight."

"But, but," Daphne started to stammer as he closed the passenger door and walked over to the driver's side.

He smirked gently and said, "Remember you asked me how I became such a good dancer?"

She nodded.

"Well, I'm going to show you." He started the car and made his way back into downtown Santa Lucia.

All the way back into town, although she wasn't the worrying type, Daphne was fretting and working out where they were going. Daniel laughed and continued to reassure her she was dressed just fine, so gorgeous it didn't matter where they'd be. She'd be the belle of the ball.

He kept driving past the downtown core, up near the freeway, but not quite to the industrial or seedy outskirts. He pulled the car to a stop outside a long, one-story building with a flashing neon sign. "Here we are!"

Daphne studied the sign. It was blinking and moving with red, white and blue lights. They lit up a rolling ball, then pins, then exclamation points with the words 'Strike it Lucky Bowling Lanes.' She gave him a look of disbelief. "Bowling?"

"Yes, bowling," he replied. "I was State 10-pin Champion when I was twelve. The dancing lessons helped give me balance and form. I haven't bowled in years, but I always remember how much fun it was. I gave up the sport when I realized I'd meet more girls at dances. It made my mother happier, too. She thought it was a much better activity for the son of a horse breeder."

She looked at him, a tad flummoxed as she went through her own personal history. "You know, I don't think I've ever bowled in my life!"

"Well, they don't have an alley at the yacht club, that's for sure. Come on, I have a reservation and if we don't take it, they'll give the lane to someone else."

"But aren't there balls and special shoes?" She looked down at her black stiletto patent leather pumps as he helped her out of the car.

"Oh, they'll have all that. We can rent them. I'm sure they'll even have a pair to match your dress." As he took her hand, she gave her head a little shake, shrugged her shoulders and started to laugh. Daphne, the good sport that she was, was ready to play.

The clatter and roll of the lanes was competing for noise with the Elvis that was blaring over the PA system, and players were jeering and cheering. The joint was jumping. It made Daphne feel happy with all the activity around after such a somber and tense day. They went to the counter to pick up their shoes and find out their lane number. She tried to hide her momentary dismay when she realized he was serious when he told her that the shoes were used and rented, not newly purchased and hers alone. They felt a little moist and warm but she was determined not to be in any way disagreeable to her currently favorite date.

She sat down at the curved bench seating, looking out on the lanes and saw the table contraption directly in front of her. "What's this?" she asked.

"It's how we keep score. Don't worry; I'll take care of that part." She'd seen bowling in magazines and on television and in movies, but seeing all the action and motorization of the ball returns and pinsetters had her mesmerized.

"Okay, how do we start?"

"First things first; I'm ordering a beer. Want one?"

Daphne rarely had beer. She didn't think they even served it at the club, or at home for that matter. But when in Rome, why not? "Yes, I will!"

"Good. Cheeseburger and fries as well? We can eat while we play." He signaled over to a waitress and ordered for them.

They began to bowl. She had laughed heartily as her wide crinoline skirt kept flouncing up when she tried to roll the ball down the lane, using two hands. Her movements also had to be very strategic, because even though her halter was well constructed, side slippage had to be kept in check due to the athletic maneuvers. Towards the end of the first game, she was able to occasionally avoid the gutters and fluked out on the second game with a strike and a spare.

They stopped to eat and she couldn't believe how good the cold beer and cheeseburger with fried onions tasted. She forgot all about what she thought the evening was going to be. She set her burger down and had a good, long look at Daniel. He was so at ease in so many places.

He met her eyes as he dipped a fry in ketchup. "Having a good time?"

"Honestly?" she continued their gaze.

Daniel paused momentarily, a little wary. "Yes."

"I'm having a great time!"

He was relieved. "I wasn't sure at first; you seemed a bit uncomfortable."

She opened up her mouth, about to do what she'd done in the past and what her mother had taught her to do—reassure her man about her feelings about him and the things he did, even if it was a white lie. Then she closed her mouth, kept in his gaze and decided to be honest and tell him the truth. "I was a little disappointed at first. After such an enchanting time at the ball, I was hoping we were going out dancing again." She looked down at her dress pleased to see she hadn't spilled anything on it yet. "I even wore one of our new holiday gowns. You should have seen the first one I picked out, a long formal version. Thank God Margot talked me into this one." She took another bite of her burger, set it down and chewed, watching his face register a slight downturn. "But I have to admit, I'm really enjoying myself tonight. You always keep me guessing at who you really are. Thank you."

Daniel perked up again, his blonde bangs flopping down just so, making him adorable with a dopey grin on his face. She reached over and touched his cheek, giving him a kiss.

Their romantic bliss was disrupted when out of the corner of her eye, Daphne spied Irene and Eddie in a far lane. She moved her head back and Dan looked over her shoulder to follow her line of sight. Irene saw them as well and there was no way that they could not acknowledge each other without being completely rude. She gave a little wave and Irene nodded at her, but made no effort to come over.

As they were finishing up, Daphne excused herself to the ladies' room. While she was powdering her nose, Irene joined her at the mirror. It was a little awkward at first, but it was clear that Irene wanted to talk. Daphne broke the ice. "So, how's your evening?"

"I've had better. You?" Irene was touching up her blood red lipstick, meeting her gaze in the mirror's reflection.

"Actually, we're having a terrific time. I had no idea bowling would make such a great date!" Irene said nothing in return, just primped her dark locks into place. Daphne decided that directness was the best approach. "What happened this afternoon?"

"What do you mean?"

"When the police questioned you. You were so quiet after you spoke with them."

Irene shrugged, not saying a word, but making no effort to go away either. Daphne gave the room another look around and seeing that it was still just the two of them, continued. "Come on, Irene. They said something to you or something happened. You'll feel better if you talk about it and I won't say anything." *Well,* she thought, *not to anyone other than Margot and maybe Daniel, but they don't count.*

Irene rolled her eyes, took a sigh and started. "We were the last ones to be with Efrem before the murder."

"Why is that so bad?"

"Horace told the cops he overheard us talking about the necklace."

"Who's Horace?"

"Runs the bar. Bud's. Owns it, actually."

"What about Bud?"

"There's no Bud."

"Then why is it called Bud's?"

Exasperated, Irene snapped. "How should I know? Anyway, Eddie made some lame remark to Efrem while he was sitting at the bar with Dirk about how I'd be his girl if he could have the rocks that Efrem had with him. I told him off but he and Efrem were just blabbing at each other. It meant nothing but I guess it was enough to give them something to go on."

The girls were silent while another woman came and went. Then Irene continued. "They wanted to search my grandmother's house."

"Oh, no! What did you do?"

"I told them no—they'd have to get a warrant or something. Look, what I get up to is my own trouble, but they have no right to tear her house upside down over nothing!"

"What happened then?"

"They said if they needed to they would." Irene paused, visibly rattled, more so than Daphne had ever seen her.

"Well, that's okay. If you've got nothing to hide and they do search, then you'll be in the clear. Wouldn't that be better?"

"Yeah," she sighed, "but it would still upset her." Irene might bend her curfew rules, but she was fiercely protective of her grandmother. "And cops can twist things, even your friend Tom's not above that. Look, it was all just talk. Eddie trying to impress me; there's nothing about it. I'm not involved and I don't want to be."

"What about Eddie?"

"What about him?"

Daphne persisted. "Do you think he's involved?"

Irene shrugged. "He's got his fingers in a lot of pies."

"Is it a good idea for you to be going with him?"

"I can take care of myself." She gave Daphne the once-over and raised her eyebrows at her appearance. "What happened to you? Did the yacht club burn down?"

Daphne forgot she was dressed in semi-formal attire while the rest of the crowd was in jeans and chinos. She laughed at Irene's remark. Even though it was somewhat rude, it was typical Irene and she felt a sense of relief as she realized her employee was back in her usual form. "Daniel's plans are unpredictable. This was a bit of a surprise but actually we're having a great time. I never knew bowling was so much fun!"

"Yeah, good family fun," she sneered. "Eddie's lawyer told him to stay out of the bar and away from the track and be seen in public doing wholesome things. He was told to bring a date, so here I am."

The two women said their good-byes and departed. Daniel was waiting for her at the counter where they exchanged their shoes. She told him about her conversation with Irene when they were in the car.

"She does get herself involved in some interesting circumstances," he remarked. "Hope she doesn't drag her grandmother in along with her if she gets in over her head. Eddie could be bad news."

"Irene seems very self assured. She says she knows nothing about Efrem and the necklace."

Daniel hesitated before he spoke and then continued. "She could also have a reputation that's not good for Poppy Cove."

Daphne felt a spur of defensiveness. "She does a good job for us, and beyond that, it's her own business."

He backed off, changing the conversation as he pulled out of the parking lot. "The one fellow I feel is getting a rough deal is Efrem Goldberg."

Daphne agreed. "It's hard to believe that someone that Betty knows would be a cold-blooded murderer."

Daniel agreed. "He seems too laid back for that kind of thing."

"I'd like to think so too, but you should have seen him at the store. He got so riled up!"

They came to a stoplight and he turned to face her. "What do you mean? When was he at the store?"

Daphne blushed and put her hand to her mouth. In all the excitement, she forgot that Daniel would know nothing about Efrem's discovery and ensuing panic. Realizing that maybe she was spilling the beans, but had gone too far to take it back, she began to tell him all she knew after swearing him to secrecy.

By the time she'd finished, Daniel was pulling into a spot along the beach. After he turned the car off, he thought for a moment before speaking. "He must have been really panicked to act in that way. He's certainly different from the Efrem I knew."

"Knew? You knew him?" She gave him a quizzical look. "How? Didn't you just meet him Saturday night?"

"No," Daniel replied. "I remembered earlier this week that I'd met them at the spa. He and Rebecca were there on their honeymoon." Dan was referring to the spa up in Ojai that he had worked at prior to his position at the Academy.

Daphne chuckled softly, recollecting how he'd run into Constance up there, prior to her murder. "Is there anyone you haven't met in Ojai?"

He reached over and pulled her closer. "Yes, you." He gave her an embrace and kissed her head. "Now why don't we forget all about necklaces and murder and enjoy how beautiful you look in the moonlight?"

"Why not? If I can bowl in this dress, a few grains of sand and a splash or two aren't going to hurt me!" She grinned as she eagerly took off her heels while Daniel came around and opened the door. He took her hand and the pair took their time strolling out in the enchanted night.

CHAPTER ELEVEN

"He took you bowling?" Margot swallowed her coffee before allowing her smirk to go to a full-blown laugh. The girls were sitting upstairs at their desks going through the morning tasks.

"Yes!" Daphne was amused by her friend's reaction.

Margot's mind carried on through the image, picturing Daphne rolling a gutter ball, elegantly trying to keep her crinolines down and halter-top up, all the while in rented shoes. "In what you were wearing? How did you manage?"

"Just fine. We had a great time, to be honest. I've never done that and we had fun." Margot continued to laugh, causing Daphne to become a little indignant and defensive. She straightened out a stack of papers with more force than she meant to. "I'd go again, too."

"Well, it certainly was an unexpected date. At least you weren't in the floor-length formal! Maybe next time he could give you some clue as to what you're doing so you could at least dress for it." Although Margot meant it as just conversation, it struck a nerve in Daphne.

"Daniel just wanted to show me how he became such a good dancer." She explained how he went from a champion bowler to tripping the light fantastic.

Margot was a little skeptical. "He's full of surprises, isn't he? I mean, when he saw how you were dressed, he must have known you were expecting more of an occasion." She stopped shuffling papers and looked at Daphne.

"No, I was fine with it. He had an idea of what he wanted to do and went ahead with it." She broke into a smile again. "You know, he's the first man I've ever dated who's been so unpredictable. We even had beer!" She got lost in thought about all the dates she'd been on in the past; they'd been so typical—always going to the right clubs, proper dinners, expectations of behavior met, but not exceeded. The first time *they* went out together was a horse ride in the hills that turned into a champagne picnic at sunset. And that was in denim and checked shirts.

Daphne's private thoughts were lost on Margot, who was busy organizing swatches for both winter and spring orders. "Don't get me wrong," she said to Daphne. "Daniel seems like a nice guy, but he's got some funny ideas about how to date." Margot and Tom's courtship had been quite normal in Margot's eyes, with a series of rather typical fancy dinners out and a movie, then eventually becoming more casual, with picnics and nights in with home cooked meals by her once they became more comfortable together, no mistaking that their intentions were of a seductive nature to each other. And she liked that. "Are you sure he's interested in you romantically? I mean, he seems to switch from courting you to treating you like a sister."

Daphne broke out in a huge grin and blushed. "There was no mistaking what was on his mind when he kissed me in the moonlight last night."

Margot shook her head pleasantly, smiling back at her friend. "Well then I stand corrected."

"I'm really happy with how things are going with him. What he does, the way he is, is so different from my usual dating habits, and that's good. It was all getting so boring."

"That's true," Margot agreed. "Except for...well, we won't go into that. That was a little more than you bargained for."

"No kidding." Daphne changed her demeanor as she thought to relate the other big news from the evening. "Say, guess who I saw last night?"

"Who?" Margot asked distractedly, more interested in some fun atomic cotton prints than playing along.

"Irene."

"Where?"

"She was at the bowling alley too, with Eddie."

"Oh, my!" Her attention shifted. "What happened?"

Daphne informed her of their conversation, telling her everything, including how Irene was rattled about her grandmother's house being under suspicion. The two continued to speculate about their take on Irene's level of involvement until they could not hash it out any further.

Betty came in for her usual 10 a.m. to 4 p.m. shift, looking a little more like herself than she had on Tuesday. She was perfectly suited for the early fall day with her perky blonde pony tail done up in a black ribbon, wearing a burgundy cashmere twin set, paired with one of the store's gray tweed circle skirts and black patent pumps. She'd been in contact with Rebecca earlier in the morning and informed her employers of all she knew before the day got busy.

Apparently, Efrem had been released from the police station but was warned to stay in town. After his alcoholic stupor had worn off, he came clean to the police, telling them all he could remember about the night of the murder. He remembered drinking at Bud's and talking to Dirk, Irene and Eddie, but had no recollection of driving to Nora's neighborhood, and did not recall going to her house. Even though he was worried about what Isaac would say, he was more concerned about being accused of theft and murder, and told the police all about the discovery of the fake necklace and how he had to get the real one back. The police had searched his and Rebecca's home and the jewelry store and had found no trace of it, and no signs he was involved in a struggle. Apparently, the scratches on his hands were all just idle gossip and conjecture. His hands were actually undamaged and unmarked. There was no physical evidence that he was the one who'd broken into Nora's room, and Efrem's own theory was that he'd fallen asleep in his car, waiting until he sobered up before he went to the Burbank's. Unfortunately, Nora had been murdered and the necklace taken from the house before that could happen. The police now believed he was telling the truth, and see his story as a distinct possibility.

"Efrem's at a real loss; he has no idea how anyone knew, other than him, about the real necklace—where it was, and how he—or she for that matter—knew to take it," Betty stated at the end of her tale.

Daphne sipped her coffee and looked in Irene's direction. She briefly shot Daphne a look, signaling her to keep their conversation from last night mum. Daphne gave a curt nod of acknowledgement. Irene put her head down and continued to fuss with the appointment book. Although the cops had not searched her grandmother's house yet, Irene knew it was still a possibility, even though Eddie had never been to her house. She didn't want to have him involved with her family. He was not that sort of date. Irene also had no idea where Eddie stood on the suspect list and didn't feel it was any of Betty's business.

Even though there was still an unsolved crime or two hanging in the air, knowing that Efrem was probably in fact innocent eased the atmosphere somewhat. The staff got busy with the day, including

Irene who was able to privately rationalize that she and Eddie were not the same people. They just knew each other. They were not in each other's back pockets. She could justify that his problems were his and none of her business. Custom appointments and new stock all took up her day, giving a sense of busy normalcy.

That was until about 2 p.m. "Looks like Poppy Cove's involved in another murder. Care to make a statement?" Michael Weathers, the dark-haired, weasely crime reporter burst in on the scene in his usual abrupt and crass manner.

Irene slyly looked down at him. He was short, about 5'6" compared to her 5'8" frame which was made taller today in her 3-inch heels. He reached to push up the bridge of his wire-framed glasses out of a suit sleeve that was too long for his build. She said nothing and walked away.

The store at the time was full of customers. The local society ladies stopped flipping the racks and admiring themselves in the mirrors while Margot went to the desk where Weathers was demanding attention. "Mr. Weathers, would you care to explain your question? I don't think we understand your insinuation."

"Well, the way I see it is that all or some of you dames were in the know or a witness to what's been going on. I'm just doing my job and all the scoops have led me here again." He flipped through his small wire-topped note pad, readying his questions. "Let's see— everyone now knows that Goldberg came here on Monday, claiming that he needed to exchange Nora's rocks on the sly; then she's murdered overnight, and the jewels are AWOL." He turned to face Betty. "You're best friends with the main suspect's wife and even though he's been shelved, he's not out of the woods yet and rumor has it he's a drunken hothead." He swiveled further to catch up with Irene. "You, you were seen with that punk hood Eddie and well-known lush Dirk Roberts, talking about what gems like that could do for them and their love lives." Now Weathers was on a roll, finally settling on Daphne. "And, you had to stop a near violent princess catfight where Nora's ex and rival were accused of wrong doing by name." He clipped his notebook shut in triumph, just beginning his inquisition. The shoppers stopped in their tracks, waiting for details.

Margot's dress created a presence in her wake as she sailed directly in front of the *Santa Lucia Times* crime beat reporter. She was in a crisp cotton dress with three-quarter-fitted sleeves, a slim boat-necked bodice that had self-covered buttons down the back and a gathered full skirt in majestic purple. Not being one to lose her cool, she firmly and quietly let him know his behavior was not to be tolerated in her place of business and no comments would be made from her or the rest of the staff. Daphne was a couple of paces behind her, assuring their clientele that all was fine, smiling and addressing the ladies. Irene began tending to the dressing rooms, guiding the clients to their occupied spaces, and Betty offered refreshments to the rest of the shoppers.

A few silent, tense moments followed. The tenacious bulldog didn't want to give up any bones, but the girls weren't giving anything away either. Eventually Weathers gave up, feeling outnumbered when the loyal customers started to turn on him as well. He left in a frustrated huff as quickly as he'd come in. Shopping resumed, along with a healthy dose of gossip, fueled by the uninvited visitor. Mrs. Morgan and Mrs. Marshall compared rumors of Dirk's philandering with many a floozy, while others eyed Irene with suspicion due to her wild associations.

Later, in the quiet moments as the day progressed, Margot recalled how Daphne had not given her the details of the princess fight. "It was a good one," Daphne commented as she recalled the conversation. "It seemed to be about a couple of things. Caroline accused Mary Ann of wanting to kill Nora for the Miss Santa Lucia title, along with rivaling affections of a young man named Ralph, supposedly Nora's boyfriend."

"Would that be the fellow that Nora had been seeing over the summer?"

"Yes! That must be the one. Caroline even went so far as to suggest that Ralph may have stolen the necklace for her."

"Holy cats! Do you think there's any truth in that?"

Before Daphne could answer, the telephone jingled. It was Loretta on the other end. The police were done investigating Nora's remains and a funeral was set for 3 p.m. tomorrow and would be announced in the morning Times.

CHAPTER TWELVE

All the flags in Santa Lucia flew at half-mast out of respect for the passing of the reigning queen. The mayor was set to speak at the service and it seemed as though the entire population was going to attend the funeral to be held at the Community Church.

The girls decided to keep Poppy Cove open until 1:30 and then close for the day to allow the employees to attend the funeral if they so desired. Sales of any somber garments were so brisk that they ran out of anything black, navy and gray on the sales floor, leaving them nothing in their sizes to choose from for themselves. Both Margot and Daphne realized they both wore to work the same dresses that they were had been donned in just a short time ago for the funeral of their dear friend Constance. Margot's was a black demure dress with a slim calf-length skirt and a short trapeze jacket. She had a matching small hat with a dotted veil. Daphne had on a navy linen shirtdress with a tied fabric belt nipping in her waist and short sleeves. She had a small cloche hat that was worn close to the head and kept her curly hair in check.

Daphne joined her family at the church. All but her sister Lizzie and sister-in-law Grace attended, with Lizzie staying in classes for the afternoon and Grace being so far along in her pregnancy that the doctor did not believe it was wise for her to subject herself and the baby to such emotional strain. Daniel, as a faculty member of the private Stearns Academy whose population was mainly non-Santa Lucians, did not attend as he was still working. Margot sat with the Huntington-Smythes. Even though Tom was at the service, he was in full uniform on behalf of the police force. It was a double presence; he was there as a municipal representative and also to keep an eye out for possible suspects. The couple acknowledged one another and agreed to see each other later.

Betty and Dwight showed up with Efrem, Rebecca and Isaac. Efrem stood tall amid the stares and whispers of the crowd. Although the new resident had been released from police custody and cast in a more innocent light, the general Santa Lucian opinion was wary. Irene came with her grandmother and ignored Eddie when he tried to speak to her. Inappropriately dressed in his greaser jeans, white t-shirt and leather jacket, he slithered out before the ceremony.

Both Caroline Parker and Mary Ann Rutherford, unadorned in simple black dresses, came in with their parents. They acknowledged each other with polite gestures and their parents kept them apart. The situation changed as soon as a certain young man approximately their age came in alone, slouching in an ill-fitting but appropriately colored suit. Mary Ann broke free of her parents' grasp and sat beside him, linking her arm through his limp one. Caroline visibly shuddered and looked the other way, apparently disgusted that Mary Ann had the nerve to glom onto Nora's supposed ex-boyfriend, Ralph Johnson.

The last to arrive before Pastor Gregory was to start the service were Dr. Edward and Tina Burbank. They seemed to have aged ten years in the last few days. Always known as such a happy little family, the young, handsome dentist with his beautiful petite wife and pretty little daughter were the ideal Santa Lucians. Often the couple could be seen strolling around, arm in arm, tall, tanned and confident with wide, white smiles on their faces, but today, they could barely support each other to the front pew, unaware of the sad pitying glances of their fellow residents.

The Burbanks had been married for twenty-two years, living all of that time in their current town. After graduating from dental school in San Francisco, Dr. Edward married Tina, his sweetheart of four years. The two set out on a new adventure, making their home and his dental practice. She was a devoted housewife; an emotional and domestic support to her husband, active community member and had become a mother to their darling daughter Nora three years into their marriage. In the meantime, he had built his practice to be the most successful one in Santa Lucia, responsible for the care and bright smiles of prominent socialites and their families.

However, nary a smile could be seen today. There were no loud outbursts or uncontrolled wailings, save for the whole bodily sigh coming from Tina as she saw the photograph and sash draped across the pure white casket. The mood was exhausting for all who attended. The church had been packed to the rafters with those closest to the Burbank family with additional mourning townsfolk outside waiting to pay their respects in the heavy, oppressive fog that rolled in for the duration.

Only the immediate family and most intimate of acquaintances went to the cemetery for the internment. The rest of the crowd headed to the yacht club. It had been chosen for the reception as the turnout was as populous as expected and the Burbank residence was still considered a crime scene. Loretta and Jake were quietly at a corner table, making notes of who was there, whom they were talking to and whom they could tastefully feature in her column for the next day. Out of respect for the family, Jake had left his camera at home, as they had decided to use photos they had on file of select persons. The irony was not lost among the social set, as there were murmurings to the appropriateness of the venue, being that Nora had been the star of the evening in that very location just a few days ago. That night had been filled with candlelight, wine and roses with the very best Santa Lucians in their colorful gowns and sparkling adornment, swaying to the sounds of a full orchestra. Now the crowd was virtually the same, but much more somber and low-key in their funereal attire and the stark light of day, shrouded by overcast skies.

Nancy Lewis, as usual, paid no heed to the expected niceties that were required in the situation. With her husband Andrew, the bank manager, by her side, and daughter Barbara flanking the other, Nancy made various comments regarding her opinion of the latest tragic events. "All I know is that if my Barbara had run for the pageant, she would have won. None of this would have happened."

Andrew sipped his drink and excused himself from the small circle of his wife's peers that he found himself surrounded by. Nancy carried on to whoever would listen, which included Margot, Daphne and Daphne's mother Patricia. "Yes, my Barbara would have been the ideal queen," Nancy confirmed with a proud tug of her jacket peplum.

Barbara, however, was visibly uncomfortable at her mother's over-confident remarks. She was the right age to have competed in the pageant but was not carrying on in her post-secondary education, which was required for the contestants. She quietly stood back with her shoulders hunched. She looked wan and pale in a faded, shapeless black sack dress, which was obviously not purchased from Poppy Cove, but from off the rack elsewhere, as it was tight and loose in all the wrong places. Her mother gave her a sharp elbow jab to the ribs along with a hiss. "Babs" responded with a jolt, spilling her drink on herself but becoming more upright.

"Barbara is the epitome of grace and poise. Plus, she has the time to attend all of the functions without a fuss or bother, and open to any of the diplomatic escorts who would need to accompany her to any function." In other words, Babs was doing nothing with her life at the moment. She had barely finished private secondary education at Lord's on the eastern seaboard. The recommendation from the guidance counselors of the school was to marry her off to a wealthy man who could afford domestic help as soon as possible.

The social set nervously twittered and sipped at their drinks. Elaine Stinson, the Mayor's wife, caught the eye of Dr. Browning's wife, Sarah, and they both looked away from each other. Margot glanced around the room trying to spot Tom, while Daphne and Patricia dared not look at each other for fear of inappropriate reactions to Nancy's remarks, such as a fit of the giggles. Mrs. Morgan and Mrs. Marshall shared a snigger, while obviously thinking the same thing. Poor Babs Lewis wasn't exactly homely, but she wasn't doing anything to help improve her appearance either. Henpecked and nagged by her mother, she was often sullen and simpering, never seen around town on a date or at any social functions unless dragged around by Nancy. Her younger twin sisters, Betsy and Anita, were far more lively and outgoing. They were finishing their final year at Lords. Nancy was very pleased with them as they followed her advice. They took care in their presentation and how they were seen in the public eye.

"Oh, Isaac, there you are!" Nancy flitted off in the direction of the elderly jeweler and his daughter and son-in-law, who were still in the company of Betty and Dwight. Barbara stood uncomfortably in the circle until her mother took a step back and hauled her by the arm toward the new group. "The fastener on one of my new earrings won't hold." Nancy gestured to her left earlobe, indicating the new dangling diamonds that Andrew had purchased for her from Mendelson's recently. She was very proud of Andrew—it only took four trips passing by the window with him to get him to surprise her with what she wanted. "When can you fix it?"

The little old man glanced in her direction, mildly taken aback by her abrupt greeting, somewhat befuddled by her request. Isaac stood about 5'5," a titch shorter than Nancy and looking worn out and sad in respect for the day. Efrem replied for him. "Bring them by tomorrow, Mrs. Lewis. I'll have a look at them."

She gave Efrem a fleeting and dismissive glance. "Isaac, will you be in?"

"Yes, yes, Mrs. Lewis, but Efrem will take care of that for you. His hands are steadier than mine these days," he commented as he reached out to pat hers.

"Well, we'll see about that. Barbara! Where is your father?" The Lewis ladies went off to find Andrew.

"Thank you for that, Isaac," Efrem gratefully replied.

Isaac harrumphed as he looked up at his towering son-in-law. He may have been willing to save face for the business in public, but he was still angry about the use of the necklace in the fashion show and the subsequent issues that had followed. Deep down in his heart he did believe his Rebecca's husband was a good man and innocent of the crime. However, completely forgiving and trusting him with the business would definitely take time, not only from him personally, but also from the entire community. "You must listen to me. When I tell you something, ask you not to do something, how to talk to a customer, you must do as I say. I know these people; I know this town. If you want to take over, you do as they want, not as you want, capiche?"

Efrem met his father-in-law's gaze, nodded his head and Isaac knew he was right. Rebecca patted her husband's arm as she addressed her father. "Yes, Papa, he knows and he's sorry. Right, honey?" She looked up at her husband's eyes, pleading silently for his agreement. The tension dissipated as the two men let the moment pass. "Good." Rebecca grinned and slipped her arm from Efrem's, looking at her friend Betty for reassurance that she'd done the right wifely thing. Betty gave her a nod, while Dwight finished off his second sandwich.

There was an audible hush as Dr. and Mrs. Burbank had arrived. For what felt like an eternity, no one moved or said a word, unsure of how to proceed. Mayor Stinson and his wife were the first to approach them. He gripped Edward on the shoulder, shook his hand and gave Tina a light embrace.

The murmurs picked up again as the couple began to receive the attention of the crowd, only to be outdone by an outburst near the buffet table. "And I say you should just leave him alone!" The usually demure Caroline Parker was involved in her second public altercation of the week, and again it was with Mary Ann Rutherford.

"It's none of your business. Stay out of it!" Mary Ann had a punch glass in her hand, getting into a throwing position.

Ralph Johnson, not only figuratively this time, but literally was in between the two princesses. He tried to settle both ladies down but to no avail. Caroline stepped closer to Mary Ann. "You have some nerve being here with him!"

Their parents were nowhere to be seen at the moment and no one wanted to step in, captivated by the exchange. "I can show up anywhere with anyone I want. Besides, Ralph is grieving and I just want to help ease his mind, that's all." Mary Ann set her drink down and linked her arm with the boy who stood there unsure of what to do. She took the sweeter than honey approach, trying her best to make herself appear as the better one in the discussion.

Caroline wasn't having any of it. She let her emotions topple her composure. "It's not right. Nora would have been so upset if she could see what was happening right now!" Her teeth were gritted and eyes tearing.

"Nora? Why would my seeing Ralph have anything to do with her?" The entire room stopped in reaction to Mary Ann's venomous and ill-placed remark.

"Why you..." Caroline couldn't speak anymore and picked up a nearby handful of shrimp puffs, ready to lodge them into Mary Ann's face. Mary Ann picked up her glass.

"Now ladies, this isn't..." Dirk, in full announcer mode and take charge swagger, stepped into the fray, just in time to get pummeled with the lobbed food and beverage, each girl meant for the other.

Tom, in uniform with the rest of his staff, made their way forward and broke up the altercation. The respective parents of the two girls rushed to their sides, pulling them apart and assuring the police that there was no need for further action; they would keep the girls apart. Ralph snuck away and Dirk excused himself to get cleaned up. Loretta nudged Jake, making sure he'd also taken everything down so they could compare notes later and decide what they could and couldn't use for the society page. Nancy could be heard as the Lewises left saying something to the effect that the

Danish royalty they were related to, the Rosenbergs, behave so much better than any common town princesses. Andrew was behind his two women and could be seen visibly shaking his head at his wife's condescending remarks.

CHAPTER THIRTEEN

"Well, that was some event!" Daphne commented as she sipped her martini. Daniel had joined her, along with Tom and Margot after work at Chelli's for a drink and a nibble. They informed him of the day's events.

"For a few minutes, I thought we'd have to step in as reinforcements," Tom remarked.

Margot laughed. "Those two are certainly behaving badly."

"Fine representatives for your town," Daniel added. "Santa Lucia would be better served as Mr. Anthony being the queen!"

The group all let off a little steam at the idea of the well-known beautician wearing a tiara and sash, toddling around town in kitten heels, blowing kisses to his adoring public. It was common knowledge that the man, although long married to a rather mannish battle-axe, had a taste for the frillier aspects of life, and was often called in to help train the pageant winners how to act like ladies.

Daphne's curiosity got the better of her. By the time the antipasto platter arrived, she could not resist any further. "So, how is the investigation going? Can you tell us anything?"

Tom looked her squarely in the eyes, took a sip of Chianti, pausing for a long minute. "You know I can't say anything." He looked over at Margot for reassurance, but instead was met with the same inquisitive look. He rolled his eyes and stayed firm.

"Not a word." At least Daniel was giving him a look in agreement.

Daphne's beau backed him up. "Come on, ladies, give the man a break. The last time you got involved, you even had me as a suspect and I don't want that happening again." He smiled, doing his best to keep it light.

"But we are involved," Margot reasoned. "From what we know, this all started with the necklace, and Efrem dragged *us* into this. We didn't want to have anything to do with it."

"That's right," Daphne continued, listing all the points of how they were involved. "Efrem wanting to do the exchange of the necklaces at the store, the fight of the princesses," she looked to her business partner for encouragement.

Margot carried on. "One of our employees knowing the first main suspect and another one possibly connected with another, even getting her grandmother mixed up in it all. My God, it's starting to sound like *Peyton Place*."

Daphne nodded excitedly and digressed. "Oh, yes! I've read in *Silver Screen* magazine that there's a movie coming out of it," referring to the novel that had come out the previous year. It had created quite a buzz.

"I've heard Lana Turner's in the lead role," Margot continued.

"Did you know that Joyce Jones was up for the part of Allison, but she turned it down," Daphne added.

"Really?"

"Yes, I overheard her talking about it to her assistant when they were here. It didn't make sense to me at the time, but now I know what it was about," Daphne confirmed. "There was some kind of scheduling problem with the Miss Starfire appearances."

Margot recollected the star's recent visit to Santa Lucia and her impromptu fashion show that had Poppy Cove all atwitter on a sad Saturday afternoon. "She was really nice. I hope she comes back."

Daphne nodded. Tom harrumphed and she looked at him. "Oh, right." She became more professional. "Face it, Tom. Whether you like it or not, we're involved, so I think we have a right to know. It could affect our business."

Margot's brows went up, liking the way her business partner was thinking. She linked her arm with Tom's and smoothed his shoulder, looking at him in a soft and appealing way. "There must be something you can tell us, give us some indication of who's involved or innocent. Anything?"

Daniel in the meantime sat back and watched the show. Tom gave it some thought, ran his hand over his wavy dark hair, sighed and said, "There's a lot more to the case than any of you know about." He firmly crossed his arms, not removing Margot's from his, but his jaw was set tight, not ready to give over any more information.

"So, if we guess, can you tell?" Daphne sparked at the hint.

"No." Tom's statement was flat and determined.

"What about having to speak the whole truth and nothing but the truth, so help you God?" Daphne pursued.

"Since when is a table at Chelli's the witness stand?" Tom gave a chuckle, while Daniel outwardly laughed and Margot rolled her eyes. "I don't have to tell you anything!"

"But you'd like to, right?" When he didn't answer, Daphne paused and took another tack. "What about Margot? Don't you want her, and our business, for that matter, to be safe? There must be something you can tell us; we know everyone who's a suspect, for goodness' sake!"

"All I can really say is that you should stay out of it and tell Irene and Betty to do the same as well. And don't invite the princesses to the shop together."

"Ooh, are they suspects, too? What about Ralph?" Daphne continued.

"Maybe, but I was thinking more with the girls that you don't want them to cause any more damage to your stock," he remarked, with a grin. "I do mean it, though. No one's been dropped from the suspect list yet and if anyone is caught up in something they don't know about, they could still be an accessory, whether *they* think they are innocent or not. Have I made myself clear?"

Margot patted his arm, wanting to move on, knowing when he was done with a topic. She did not want to aggravate her man, as it would make for an unpleasant evening of cold shoulders. Daphne, however, felt she was on a roll and kept going. "Yes, G-man, loud and clear, but just one more thing."

He blew out an exhausted air and then indicated with a gesture for her to continue.

"Right," she said, after given permission for one more niggle. "Do they have any leads on the real necklace? Where is it and is it actually the motive for the murder?"

"First of all, that's more than one question. All I'll tell you is that it's still at large and no one is exempt from guilt. Now if you don't mind, I'd like to order some spaghetti and enjoy the rest of the evening, including the fine company that the Daphne who minds her own business can provide." He reached across the table and tweaked her nose, just to show there were no hard feelings. They all laughed and the rest of the dinner went splendidly, so much so that when it was time for Tom to say good night to Margot when he took her home, he didn't. His car was parked in front of her house the next day, which left her neighbor, Mrs. O'Leary, to wonder how early he must have come over in the morning—or if he'd been there all night.

CHAPTER FOURTEEN

Being that it was a Saturday morning, it was lively even though it was the day after the funeral. Just outside the front door of Poppy Cove on Avila Square was the weekly Farmer's Market where all the local growers brought their finest produce and flowers. People mingled and moved to the sound of a mariachi band, and shopped, catching up on all the latest gossip. The biggest topic of the day seemed to be Loretta's article in the *Times*. In her column, she announced that Mary Ann Rutherford would be promoted to the position of Miss Santa Lucia Queen, and Caroline Parker would be first princess with a vacant second princess post for the rest of the term. In addition, Loretta decided to write an editorial regarding both of the royalty choices and the future of the pageant altogether. She spoke out about the public displays of bad behavior of the two remaining court attendants and ended with a plea of concern regarding the behavior of young girls in modern times.

Everyone seemed to have something to say about the matter, including Mr. Anthony who came over to the store in a flouncy huff. "Well, I hate to say it, but that Miss Simpson may be right." The diminutive blond man with hair a little finer at the top of his crown than he wished for, carried on in his palaver. "These girls, I tell you, they're getting more unruly every year." Deportment was another of Mr. Anthony's forays, second only to his talent of perfecting the most glorious hairstyles in town. He stopped his aimless ranting in his tracks when he saw Margot, who was busy fixing a sash on the white blouse of a new client. "Oh dear, what happened here? Did we have a bad night? I can't believe you've been out in public like that! No matter, I'll fix it now." As always, he had a can of hairspray in one hand and a brush in the other.

Margot had no idea what he was talking about, as he made his way forward, interrupting her with a new customer, who looked as bewildered as she did. Daphne and the rest of the staff stopped what they were doing and watched him approach her, confused as to what the fuss was about. As Margot turned to face him, he inadvertently shot a spritz of hairspray at her, just missing the customer. "Mr. Anthony, what are you doing?"

"Dear, it's for your own good. As always, you are impeccably dressed, right down to those fabulous new red shoes, but the back of your head, darling, well, that just won't do!" He began teasing out a small, flat spot at the back of Margot's brunette crown that wasn't as lively as the right side, alternating spritzes and brushstrokes. The hair faux pas was so slight that no one had even noticed it—before him, that is.

Margot *had* left in a bit of a hurry after sleeping in and saying a fond farewell to her companion. She consciously ignored the stares from her nosy neighbor. She was getting used to it, as it wasn't the first time Mrs. O'Leary had tried to keep tabs on her visitor's arrivals and departures. She thought she had left looking fine, everything in place. She was wearing a new slim-fitting charcoal gray tropical wool day dress, that had three-quarter French-cuffed sleeves, double breasting with red piping and accessorized with a matching red belt and pumps. She felt especially natty today with a Julia Mackay pocketbook that carried the gray and red-piped theme. Both Tom and Mr. Cuddles the cat had been suitably impressed. In her once-over, she noticed her eyeliner was smudged in just the right way and she had no lipstick on her teeth. She thought her pageboy was fine, from the front, anyway.

"There, that's so much better," Mr. Anthony remarked, then twirled around the room, looking for other fashion victims. "See what I mean about the youth of today? No, that will never do. Frizz is the sign of neglect!" He moved onto poor Abigail Browning, the weekend help. She was bewildered as he approached the sides of her head, smoothing out what she had pulled back in a perky swinging ponytail, ideal for her sixteen-year-old face. The girls could not figure out if she was offended or just stunned and rushed over to help her handle the hair attack.

"Come near me with those things and you won't have arms," Irene glared at him.

He backed a step away. "No, no, you're fine. The mane is perfection, but I must say, the lipstick's a little too nighttime for daywear. Now I'm not the expert, that's Todd's area, but I'm sure he'd say the same thing if he were here."

"There you are! Why did you leave? You've got Mrs. Francis sitting in a rinse!" Todd came over to get him.

"Well, I had to talk about the future of the pageant. Mrs. Francis just showed me the article in the *Times* and I was beside myself. These ladies are the only beauty experts I could find at the moment," indicating the shop owners. "You were busy and I was so upset!" He paused for a moment, his bottom lip trembling. "The pageants are my passion. I just don't know what I'll do if they cancel them."

There was an awkward silence while everyone in the shop considered how to console him. Finally, Todd put his arm over his employer's shoulder and turned him around to lead him out the door. "Now, now, you know if you leave a blue rinse on too long it goes purple. Remember the last time you did that to Mrs. Francis? Let's not do that again."

"Oh you're so right," he slumped into his assistant's arms, wringing his hands. "I must persevere." He squared up his shoulders, mustering up his courage as he took a deep breath and dramatically exclaimed, "Miss Santa Lucia will continue to reign! I will personally see to that!" He shook off Todd and clicked away in his highly polished black patent brogues. Todd gave a little shrug and smiled to the girls as he followed behind Mr. Anthony.

The day was already humming along with plenty of gossip and speculation regarding the matter that had so flustered Mr. Anthony. The chatter continued with the subjects of the murder, necklace theft and the public fight at the funeral yesterday. There was a bluster at the door, as Loretta made her way in with bags of fruits and vegetables from the market. She had carrot tops spilling out from one bag and a bouquet of asters from another. "Girls, exciting news for tomorrow. Cancel your plans––we're all off to the races!"

Margot nodded and acknowledged her friend, as she was busy showing Mrs. Morgan the drape of the new red taffeta holiday skirt and how it glowed and changed shades as it flowed, while the rest of the staff continued to tend to customers as well. Loretta was a bit discouraged that no one stopped what they were doing immediately. She set her bags down on the sales desk and gave a little cough while she waited. Finally, after what seemed like an eternity to her, Daphne came over and gave Loretta her full attention.

"Now, what was this about the races?" the blonde enquired.

"Well, the town pageant committee decided that they needed to soldier on now that the funeral is over. It's a last minute thing." She paused for effect, to make sure every pair of available ears was tuned to her voice.

"The *County Cup* race is being run at the Santa Lucia County Race Track tomorrow up in Santa Ynez," she continued. "It's a good public appearance opportunity for the new Miss Santa Lucia to be introduced in society, now that poor Nora's gone." Loretta bowed her head for an appropriate show of public respect. "Miss Dairy Queen, that's Solvang's royalty, usually does the presentation, but the mayor graciously gave us the honor as a goodwill gesture. Now then, Golden Boy's running in the 5th. He's a local horse; comes from Henshaw Farms," she remarked while flipping through her notepad. "Say, isn't that Dan's last name?"

Daphne smiled, recalling what he'd told her. "Yes, sound like that's his parents' business. They raise Arabians mainly and usually for show or dressage, but I imagine some racers, too. I'm sure he'd love to go." She turned to Margot. "Let's all make a day of it—picnic, drinks. Think of it—what fun we'll have!"

Margot thought it over, feeling a bit reserved. It would be fun, but after all, they'd just attended a funeral where the murder victim would have been one of the guests of honor. "Isn't it a little soon to be celebrating with Miss Santa Lucia?"

"No, not at all!" Loretta passed off the thought with a wave of her hand, then recoiled slightly. "Well, some consideration was made. That's why they picked an event out of town, but still in the county."

Still not fully sold on the party spirit, Margot had another concern. "What about the idea that there's still a murderer on the loose and the queen was the victim?"

Loretta didn't let her spirits get dampened. "Oh, tish-tosh! There'll be so many people there in public, there's no chance of anything going wrong."

"That's Santa Lucia. God forbid that the social set gets a curfew over a murder," Irene muttered slyly as she left the sales desk and conversation.

The Society Editor decided to ignore Irene. "Weathers told me he's heard that it'll be crawling with cops—a good opportunity to catch someone in the act, so to speak, if they try anything." She surreptitiously looked around before adding more. "It's also a way they can keep an eye on Mary Ann. She's still a suspect—her and Ralph. Rumor has it they want to keep her in check, see if she was behind it all. Wouldn't it be exciting if something did happen?"

Margot frowned at the idea, but Loretta continued. "There's no safer place to be." She grabbed Margot's arm, gave it a jostle and spoke louder. "Come on, it'll be fun—everyone'll be there and I've got a bunch of passes for the VIP section from Lenny."

"Who's Lenny?" Daphne asked.

"Lenny Cohen. He's the rookie on the sports desk. It's a big deal for him; he's covering the track. It's his first big assignment." She turned back to look at Margot. So what do you say, Mar? Are you going to join the party?"

Margot thought it over and wondered if Tom would be working the event or would have the day off. Even in the middle of a case, he'd usually have Sundays free, handing off responsibility to the next in command, who would most likely be Riley. But then again, being that it was out of town, maybe another department would be handling it altogether. She had to admit a day at the races with her friends might be just the thing. Margot was already coming around to it as Daphne twisted her rubber arm.

"Think of it, Mar—a chance to wear new outfits, show off our finery to the Santa Ynez 'in' crowd. What do you say?" Daphne had been sold on the idea from the first word, already imagining what she might pick out to wear and having another reason to be out with Daniel in public, happy that they made such an attractive couple.

"Okay, let's pick out some dresses," Margot laughed as she relented. "Who's all coming to the track?"

There was a flurry of activity as the girls, joined by some of the customers, began flipping through the racks of dresses and suits, choosing bright colors and happily conversing with one another. Penny Garrett, the Police Department switchboard operator Margot had talked with the other day, came in during the excitement. When she heard about the event and how everyone was getting new outfits, she decided she wanted one for herself, even though she wasn't planning on going. She chose a teal dress in a lustrous cotton sateen that had a peter pan collar, three-quarter wing cuffs, rhinestone buttons down the front, with a fitted bodice and a wide sweeping skirt that was supported by a matching peacock crinoline that only showed when it was supposed to. It set off her auburn hair and emerald eyes, making her fair skin luminous. "Forget the races, I'm setting my sites on lining up a date for tonight!" She added a swipe of plum lipstick to her mouth, gave her curls a primp and decided to wear the dress right out the door. Penny took the outfit she'd been wearing, which was a pair of blue capris and a sleeveless mint blouse, put into a Poppy Cove bag, and made her way out the door with a wiggle and a sashay to attract her sort of man.

Daphne, Margot and Loretta looked out the picture window that faced the Avila Square fountain amidst the crowds of people and market stalls. Within a minute, a handsome man dressed in slacks and a sports shirt approached Penny as she was picking over summer squash. The shop spectators were enthralled as the couple's conversation looked so intense over the vegetables. Penny gave a smile, then a nod to the man, set down the squash, took his arm and gave a little wink over her shoulder to the girls back inside Poppy Cove.

"Incredible," Loretta muttered. "Lucky Penny!" The reporter had little if any good fortune in her own love life since moving to Santa Lucia about five years ago, after being a Hollywood gossip reporter. She never spoke much about that earlier time. She always avoided the subject—that and her past romantic adventures. For someone who made a living getting others to spill the beans, she was a tight-lipped clam.

"Yeah, hope he doesn't throw her in the fountain..." trailed off Irene as she gave the scene a passing glance.

The group had to admit that it was pretty funny and gave a round of giggles as they went back to work. Loretta was busy taking down requests for passes, while the Poppy Cove staff was busy with their clientele. Dresses, hats, gloves, purses were being tossed around from one lady to the other, including a minor debacle between Mrs. Morgan and Mrs. Marshall that was quickly defused after Abigail brought out an additional box of cotton gloves.

"Miss Simpson, could I speak with you for a moment?" Betty approached Loretta quietly.

"Oh, what? Of course, Betty. What is it?" Loretta looked up from her notes as the girl touched her elbow and the two moved to a quieter corner.

"Well, I'd like to get some passes for tomorrow, if that's okay."

"Sure, Betty! And call me Loretta. After all, we're friends, aren't we?" She'd been a little perplexed at

Betty's sudden formality and wasn't sure why she referred to her in that way.

"Oh, yes, of course we are!" Betty agreed.

"Okay then. How many do you need?"

"Four," she stated.

"Sure. So that's for you and your husband, Dwight, isn't it?" Betty nodded in response to the question. "And the other two are for...?" she inquired as she wrote down the names for Lenny.

Betty sighed before she continued, then blurted out, "Efrem and Rebecca Goldberg," a little louder than she intended. The room stopped.

"Oh." Loretta flatly stated, pen poised as she mulled over the request.

Margot had overheard the exchange and came over. "Loretta, is there a problem with the Goldbergs coming to the races with us?"

"Uh, well, um, I, I, well, I don't know," she flummoxed through her words.

Margot looked at Betty, the poor girl feeling awkward and unsure of what to do. "We all know now that Efrem's not in custody anymore, and there's certainly room for doubt in his guilt."

"The race is out of town," Loretta stated, trying to find a plausible excuse to keep the suspected murderer and thief away from the social set.

"Yes, but it's still in the county, and he's been released," Margot remarked. "Look, I wanted to call Tom and find out if he could come tomorrow. I'll just ask about Efrem, too." She picked up the heavy black receiver and dialed the station number. In a moment, she had his desk. "Tom, how are you, darling?" she demurred. She paused while he answered. "Loretta's got passes for the Santa Lucia County Cup tomorrow and most of our group are going. Can you come with us or are you one of the officers on duty?" There was a long pause again as he was talking. She looked around and then quietly spoke. "Oh."

There was a longer pause and then she blushed. "Well, Loretta did hear from Weathers and Lenny, the new sports reporter that there was going to be police presence there." She looked at Loretta, giving her a stern look. "She never said anything about it being undercover. I don't think she knew."

Loretta looked away while Margot continued and Betty waited. "No, I don't think too many people heard. It was just here at the shop." She shrugged and gave a guilty look. "Well, if you're going to be there, wouldn't it help your cover to be in the group?" After his answer, she gave a smile and nod to Loretta indicating she should write his name down on her list and replied, "No, I won't say anything more about it." She was about to hang up when she saw Betty's face. "Tom, just one more thing. Betty would like to invite the Goldberg's. Is there a problem with them being there?"

From Betty's perspective, the response seemed to take forever. "Okay, I'll let them know. Will I see you later?" The two finished their conversation and she turned to her friends.

"Well, what did he say?" Loretta jumped in.

"You're in trouble," Margot remarked.

"Oh, oh, did I say too much?"

"You weren't supposed to mention that the police were going to be there. Loretta, that was top secret."

She brushed it off. "I only mentioned it here. No one's going to pay any attention to that." She avoided Margot's look and changed the subject. "What did he say about Efrem?"

Margot turned her attention to Betty. "They can come. It's probably the best place they can be."

"Thank you, Margot! And Miss, I mean, Loretta. I know he's innocent, I just know he is, you'll see!

They're good people, he's going to fit in just fine."
Betty scampered to the phone, calling to invite Rebecca
and Efrem to the weekend's event.

"You know, there are going to be some people who
aren't going to like this," Loretta mentioned to Margot.

"Loretta, there are always some people who don't
like anything we do. If the police believe there's room
for doubt, we've got to trust that. If we don't, a
murderer could get away with the crime and an
innocent man could go to jail. Besides, as Efrem is the
one poised to take over for Isaac in the near future, he's
got to put this behind him."

"And if he's guilty and pulling the wool over our
eyes?"

"Well," Margot reasoned, "if Efrem was the one
who killed Nora, it would have been for the necklace,
not the crown of Miss Santa Lucia, as far as we know.
That would mean that the current queen and princess
would be safe from him, with or without policemen all
over the place."

"So if it wasn't him, who did it, and why, and
where's the real necklace?"

Margot looked at her friend again. They were the
same questions with no clearer answers today. "That's
up to the police figure out. Now keep this to yourself. It
can't get back to Weathers or Lenny. The law
enforcement from the entire county will be watching
the event, both in uniform and undercover." She stared
at Loretta. "I mean it. Don't repeat it."

Loretta gulped and blinked, knowing her friend was
serious. "Okay, okay, lips sealed." She glanced around
the room. "Gee, I better get something new, too! What
are you going to wear?"

"Not this, it's mine now!" Daphne came out of a
dressing room in a royal blue worsted day suit. It
consisted of a fitted pencil skirt to the knee and

matching jacket that had a wide off the shoulder open collar, coming to a deep v in the front, nipping into a double breasted waist with two sets of large jet black buttons and finished at the hip. The cuffs at mid-forearm folded back, repeating the deep cuff of the collar, and were held in place with smaller matching buttons. "And I'll take these, and this." She grabbed a pair of short black stretch velvet gloves and a black patent leather pocket book. "Oh, and I've been wanting to wear this hat!" She grabbed a black pillbox with jet beads in the netting and perched it on her blonde curls. "Well girls, what do you think?"

"Fabulous! Now what about me?" Loretta moved around, darting like a sparrow and picked up a couple of garments. "I'll be right back." She whisked off to change and was back in a flash, wearing a chocolate brown suit in light wool crepe, with a long, slitted slim skirt that finished to her mid-calf and a boxy long-sleeved jacket that had a rounded jewel collar and straight opened front. Underneath it, she had a chiffon blouse in the same hue with big cream polka dots and a soft flouncing bow at the high neckline. "I have a suede bag and spectator pumps that will match perfectly! And this!" She placed a wide brimmed brown straw hat trimmed with a cream ribbon in a trailing bow at a flattering angle on her head.

"Perfect! Just one more thing." Daphne took a wide cream patent leather belt and finished the ensemble by cinching in her waist.

Loretta caught a glimpse in the mirror. "I love it! It's fun, sporty and I can work in this. It may be playtime for you girls, but I have to cover the track for my column. I figured brown might be best to hide any dirt I might uncover. Well, track dirt, anyway. The other kind? I hope to dig up something that I can't print!" She laughed. "Now what about you?"

Both turned to face Margot and size her up for the event. As social as Poppy Cove's business was, she sometimes reached her limit of public attention and started to feel that way now. She knew that in the end it would be a great time, but as a prominent member of Santa Lucia's society and a leader of the fashion elite, all eyes would be on her. More often, she was happier sewing the seams than filling them out. She sighed and let her friends help her select her racing outfit. "These would be darling on you! Have you tried them on yet?" Loretta handed her a couple of hangers and sent her off to a change room.

Margot came out moments later, pleased with the first suggestion. It was an autumnal copper shantung silk embroidered with a scattering of red poppies that had a wide boat neck front and back, fitted through the bodice, with cap sleeves. The skirt billowed out from the narrow waist to a full circle that ended at tea length. It fit her like a dream, thanks to the right girdle she had worn under her full slip that day. She smoothed out the bodice with her hands as she looked down. "This will make it complete." Daphne handed her a wide brimmed, dark tan straw hat that complimented the sheen and tone of the dress. "A vision of fall."

"Takes me back to my childhood in Vermont," Loretta sighed. The ladies looked at themselves in their finery, pleased at a good day's work.

"Well, Irene—how about you? Are you joining us tomorrow?" Loretta enquired as she met the manager at the desk to pay for her purchase.

"You all look gorgeous, but you wouldn't catch me near that place," Irene remarked. "Not on your life."

CHAPTER FIFTEEN

There was a chill in the air with heavy coastal fog blocking out the sun as Daniel and Daphne pulled up to Margot's, shortly after ten Sunday morning, heading off to the races. "Where's Tom?" Daniel asked feeling a little outnumbered.

The girls looked at each other, unsure of what to tell him. Thanks to Loretta, both of them knew that Tom was working undercover. It was something that they should not have known, and some things were better left unsaid. "He had some things to do this morning, so he's meeting us at the track," Margot remarked nonchalantly.

Daniel nodded in response and the girls gave each other a relieved glance, happy that he didn't pursue it further. After a quick discussion, they realized they had plenty of time, as they wanted to be at the track around one. They headed to Charlie's Diner on Cove for brunch. It was busy but they were able to get a booth and sat down at a chrome and Formica table. "Is any of your family coming up to the races?" Margot asked Daphne.

"No," she replied, fiddling with her coffee cup. "Grace is due any day now, so she's staying home and Mother wants to stay with her. Dad and William have a business lunch at the club, and Lizzie, well, Mother didn't want her to come with us. She's concerned enough about her behavior that she figured Lizzie would just run wild as soon as she could get out of my sight. She was tossing around betting terms this morning and between that and the detective magazines she's been reading lately, mother's concerned. She's been trying to get her into more dainty pursuits." Daphne laughed and shook her head. "Frankly, the girl's all over the place."

Margot laughed. During a quiet lull, they glanced around the café and noticed that others were dressed up in their Sunday finery and speculated that some were coming from church and others were heading off to the track as well. While they waited for their food, Margot brought up a new topic of conversation. "Loretta told us that one of the favorites comes from your family's farm."

"So I've heard," Dan acknowledged. "Golden Boy."

"Do your parents breed many racehorses?" she continued.

"No, but a few. I've not paid so much attention in the past years." Daniel, although not abrupt, was obviously not interested in carrying on the topic. His family had taken for granted that he would stay in Ojai and take over their horse breeding business along with his brother Victor. Determined to make his own way, he had left the business amicably and still remained on good terms with his family.

Daphne took a sip of her coffee and gulped, setting her cup down. "So, are your parents going to be there today?" She hadn't met them yet and it never crossed her mind until now that they might be. She felt a little nervous.

"Probably," he replied casually. "Hey, you'll get to meet them!"

The significance of this comment to Daphne went right over his head. Margot, sitting across from her friend, smiled and touched her arm. "You'll do fine."

Daphne blustered absentmindedly. "I didn't realize! Oh, I'm not ready. The least I could have done was dress up, or something."

Margot laughed, looking at her. "You are. You're wearing a brand new outfit. You look darling!"

She looked down at herself, blushed and remembered what she had on. "Well, what do I say to them?"

"The same kinds of things I said to your parents when I met them at the ball," Daniel said, referring to the first time that he'd met the Huntington-Smythes. "It'll be fine. They already love you."

"They do? Why?"

"From what I've told them about you, of course." Daniel had his arm draped over her shoulders, not concerned over the meeting.

She looked at him curiously. "What did you tell them about me?"

He shrugged. "Just about you, your shop, what we have in common, how you like horses, what I think of you."

"And what do you think of me?" Daphne spoke without thinking. She then turned a deeper shade of red, realizing that she was being much more forward than she was told was proper, especially in a public place with an audience, even if it was Margot.

Daniel was spared from answering as the food arrived. He grinned as he reached for the salt and then dug into his plate of bacon and eggs.

Daphne picked at her food, preoccupied. Margot watched the scene as she ate and was surprised. In all the years of Daphne's active love life, she had known so many of her beaus' parents, sometimes even knowing the families before dating the men. Her very outgoing friend never seemed to lack confidence when it came to social niceties.

After breakfast they decided to take the scenic San Marcos Pass through the hills. As they climbed upward, they left behind the fog belt and headed into beautiful sunlight. The road twisted and turned, the mountain scrub smelled dry and sweet, making for a pleasant journey. On the radio, local station KESL was playing the latest hit song. "Folks, that was *Honeycomb,* the latest from Jimmie Rodgers, and my, isn't that a swell tune," the disc jockey announced. "This is Jumpin' Johnny Jenkins, spinning the discs for Dirk Roberts, who's gone off to Santa Ynez to emcee the County Cup Winner's Circle. And good luck to you, Golden Boy. I've got some serious scratch riding on your tail; so don't disappoint me, local boy. And to my good buddy Dirk, let's hope you keep your mug away from Miss Santa Lucia's one-two punch, you dig me?" *Wake Up Little Susie* took over the airwaves.

"Huh," Daphne smirked. "Sounds like the events at the funeral didn't stay quiet."

"No," Margot agreed. "Jenkins. He's new, right?"

"Yep. Sure is different from his brother."

"Who's his brother?"

"Officer Jenkins," replied Daphne. "They're a year apart. I went to school with them."

"Really?"

Daphne nodded. "I graduated with Johnny. He was always a bit of a mouthpiece. Good thing he found something to do where he didn't have to keep quiet."

"So, now we know Dirk's going to be there," Margot thought out loud.

"This should be entertaining. The whole gang's going to be there all over again," Daniel spoke, summarizing the thoughts in the air.

The rest of the trip was relatively quiet, as they were enjoying the passing view of the mountains, lake and ocean fading back in the distance. All the while, each of them wondered what was going to happen with a possible thief, murderer, even potential victim or victims floating around. The true motive for the killing was still hazy. The event could be either a gay old affair or a den of vipers. It could go either way.

By the time they'd gotten to the fairgrounds, Loretta had been running around with Lenny who knew the place like the back of his hand. He was helping her interview horse owners, jockeys, and spectators. Jake, her ever faithful photographer, had been following them around, snapping pictures, changing bulbs and film rapidly, keeping pace but careful of the damp earth and turf. She greeted the group and introduced her new companion in a blur, telling them which entrance to use for the elite grandstand and that she would join them when she could.

As the threesome went by the betting windows, Daniel gave the girls a brief rundown on how it worked and they all placed modest bets on Golden Boy in the 5th. The group made their way to the VIP area and helped themselves to the champagne and canapé refreshments that were being offered. Many Santa Lucians were already there, including Mayor Stinson and his wife in their official capacity, as well as Andrew and Nancy Lewis, along with their ever-present daughter Barbara trying her best to hide in the crowd. Every time she made an attempt to leave her mother's side, Nancy would haul her closer with a pull of her arm. Then, surprisingly, a black shadow moved its way through the crowd followed by a hushed tone. The Baroness von Eissen was clad in her usual out of date black garb. Along with her two sons, they created quite a stir in their wake as they sat down in their seats.

Dirk Roberts was his usual proud peacock self, wandering around the royal viewing area, drink in hand. His official emcee duties wouldn't occur until the winners' presentations, so he made his rounds flirting and schmoozing with every young girl of note, whenever they would deign to let him near. That included the new Miss Santa Lucia who was sitting on a raised platform, along with her princess, and Solvang's reigning Miss Dairy Queen, stoically calm and placidly grinning. Miss Dairy Queen was seated on the visiting queen's right, still on the platform but not as high or as prominent. If a person looked closely enough, they would be able to see her white-knuckled hands and gritted teeth. Ralph, the unofficial escort, was moping and sullen just off the royal area, sore that Dirk was making more time with Mary Ann than he was.

Daniel raised his arm in a wave. "Daphne, they're here!"

"Oh, my God. I think I'm going to faint," she said as she turned to Margot.

"I've never seen you like this," Margot remarked back. "What's gotten into you?"

"I know! You know what?" she whispered so only Margot could hear. "I think I love him. I really do!" Daphne let herself shine, feeling all the better for saying it out loud.

Margot broke into a huge smile. "Of course you do, Daphne. It's written all over your face! Have you told him?"

"No, I'm working on hearing it from him first. I mean, I'm pretty sure he does, but he hasn't said those three little words yet. I have a plan—I'll suggest another moonlight walk tonight after we drop you off and that should cinch it. It almost happened the other night after bowling. I was sure of it, but a big wave came in and almost knocked us over and broke the spell." Daphne bubbled on excitedly, both sure and unsure at the same time.

Daniel grabbed her hand, ready to lead her in his parents' direction. "Let's go. I'd like you to meet them."

Daphne looked at her friend pleadingly, hoping she would come along to make it easier, but Margot waved her friend off, looking in the direction of an attractive and fit middle-aged couple, eagerly awaiting their son and Daphne. There was no mistaking that Nicholas Henshaw was Daniel's father—he was just an older version of the same man. Madeline, his mother, looked at the approaching couple, eager to meet the woman who was making her son so smitten. Margot turned away, knowing that all was going to go well.

"Excuse me, miss, but a woman like you shouldn't be alone in a place like this. People may get the wrong idea about you," came a strong deep voice from behind her.

She turned around to see Tom, dressed in a checked sports coat, polo shirt and light brown slacks, looking smart but casual, blending in with the sea of people. "Oh, Tom, funny guy." She looked around for his co-workers and other than one or two uniformed police officers at the edge of the crowd, she didn't see any other cop she knew. She whispered, "Are you working, or can you stay around?"

He gave her a light kiss on the lips and replied, "Yes." Then gave her a wink.

She was baffled at first, then realized that although he was affectionate to her, his eyes were roaming, scanning the crowd. "Oh!" she said, realizing she was part of the stake out. Her heart beat a little faster, and she wasn't sure if it was because Tom was near or from the excitement of the day.

"Play along, just act like we're on a regular date," Tom said easily.

"Okay, who are we watching or looking for?" Margot was keen to be on the case.

"Me? Everyone and anything. You? The horses and what everyone is wearing. Enjoy your drink and stay out of it, darling." He was not rude but firm. "You and your friends are part of my cover, not my backup. Speaking of them, where are they?"

Margot told Tom where her friends had gone and how she'd placed a small wager on Golden Boy. "Dinner's on me if he wins!"

"I'll take you up on that." Tom gave a glance around. "See anything I should know about?"

"I thought I wasn't supposed to get involved," she remarked in a sassy tone that created a sneer on Tom's face. "No, not much, other than the Baroness making her presence known in her inherited garments, Nancy and Babs at odds as usual, and Miss Dairy Queen looking ready to dethrone the visiting royalty."

"Right." He was on constant surveillance, occasionally nodding or giving discreet gestures to various men in the crowd. Margot followed his gaze and wondered what it would be like to be a detective. As a designer and dressmaker, she studied the behavior of fabrics and lines—the curve, shape and personality of the client. She realized that she and Tom thought the same way—just about different things. She felt a comfort watching how Tom got absorbed in his work, just like she did getting lost in hers. She slipped her arm through his; supporting his cover and admired the man she loved.

Then, Margot felt Tom's body tense and his eyes go on alert. She followed his gaze and saw Betty, Dwight, Rebecca and Efrem appear. It was clear who was the cause of his focus. "Goldberg." he stated with a curt nod.

"Malone," Efrem stated, looking Tom in the eye.

Margot gulped and glanced at the rest of Efrem's party, unsure of how the conversation was going to go. "Well, then, looks like everyone's here." she added.

Betty grinned anxiously, looking for a way to keep the peace and everyone happy, in her usual manner. Glancing around, she looked at the crowd in their race day finery. "Oh, my, there are some lovely dresses here! Isn't that one of yours, Margot?"

Margot turned her head and saw a woman in her mid-thirties wearing one of her favorite dresses from last season, a cotton lawn floral, white with sprays of pink roses. "Yes, but I don't recognize her. She must be from around here." A little further on in the crowd, there was another figure that she did recognize. The lovely Joyce Jones, with her trim, petite figure and wavy blonde hair was commanding a small audience. The star of B-movie fame (her most recently released *Fall in Love* had just come out at the theaters), was with her dashing co-star Derek Strong. Margot was pleased to see she was wearing a turquoise linen fitted shift dress with matching bolero jacket that she'd purchased last month from Poppy Cove, while on a shopping spree during a publicity tour as Miss Starfire, 1957. Joyce spotted Margot from under the brim of her cream-colored straw hat and gave a wide smile and wave.

Margot waved back and Betty nodded, but no one else in their group picked up the starlet's presence. Everyone else was still feeling the tension between the cop and the suspect—Tom and Efrem. Dwight was feeling warm; he slung his suit jacket over his shoulder, squinted and pushed his sunglasses up his nose. Rebecca was quiet, keeping her arm looped through Efrem's, holding him back while he and Tom continued to stare at each other doggedly.

The crowd carried on around them while it seemed like an eternity before someone spoke again. "Glad you could make it." Tom remarked.

"Why, so you could keep an eye on me?" Efrem was so intense; Rebecca could barely hold him back.

"We're keeping an eye on you no matter where you go." Tom's words carried so much weight they cast a pall on the conversation.

Efrem relented. "I didn't do it, Tom."

"If that's the case, it will prove itself. Keep your nose clean, stay out of trouble and remain in the county. We'll sort it out."

In the air there was a loud clanking sound, followed by the ringing of a bell. The first race had begun. To everyone's relief, the tensions melted into excitement. The scent of the horses, freshly mown grass and track dirt in the air took over. As did the sounds, cheers and jeers of the spectators, pounding of hooves, more bells and announcers calling the races and winners. The sights also added stimulation to the day. There were the beautiful, lean animals flying by, the jockeys in their colorful silks, and the crowd of people in their finery, as well as casual families dressed for picnics on the lawn. The races went very quickly, and before the group knew it, the main race that everyone had come to see was on.

"Margot, over here!" She looked to see Daniel and Daphne flagging to her from the rails. "Come close to watch this one!"

It was just before the start of the 5th race, Golden Boy's big event. Tom stayed behind, keeping a bird's eye vantage point of the scene while the rest of the group scrambled down to where the action was. Daphne bubbled over with excitement, effervescing about the beautiful horse, his jockey and a mention of the Henshaws, whom she now casually referred to as Nick and Madeline, leaving Margot to guess that all had gone well in the meeting with Daniel's parents. Before they knew it, the starting gates opened and the bell went off again. The ground thundered as the group of horses, eking out their places, flew by so fast they were just a blur of colors. The announcer's voice echoed so much that it was hard to understand what was happening. Rebecca was poised in front of her husband, who muttered something unintelligible from all the background noise and took off in a flash.

"Oh my God! He won!" Daphne leaped into Daniel's arms, excitedly. "Golden Boy did it!" The announcer's voice confirmed in its layers of echoes what the crowd had just witnessed. "When can I collect my winnings?"

"Did you bet on any other races?" Daniel asked her.

"Nope. Everything I had in my purse I bet on Golden Boy to win!" she beamed.

He laughed, touched at both her whim and belief in the horse. Then he twirled her around in a breathtaking embrace exclaiming, "I love you!" He proclaimed the words loud enough for the entire world to hear.

Daphne was stunned. She had wanted to hear him say those words and had been working on her scheme to make it happen, and here he had done it—just blurted it out in front of everyone! She wondered, *did he mean it?* So she asked him.

Daniel laughed. "Of course, I do, with all my heart." With that, he pulled her close and kissed her full on the lips. "You're perfect for me!"

"Well, I do too. I mean, Daniel, I love you!" It wasn't the way she'd imagined, but the declaration thrilled her heart all the same. "So what happens now?" Daphne said, not sure she meant to say it out loud, but there it was.

"For now we either keep watching the remaining races or go collect your winnings, Mrs. Rockefeller." He continued with a sly grin, "Later, I'm sure we'll figure out what to do next."

"Oh, right, yes." Daphne remarked, suddenly remembering where they were and about her winnings.

"You look like you could use some air. I'll get us some drinks. Why don't you and Margot go collect your purse? Do you have your card?"

Daphne rummaged through her handbag and found her betting slip and waved it in the air. She looked at Margot who'd been in earshot the entire time and who returned her goofy grin, happy to see such glee on the lovebirds' faces. "Come on, let's go," Margot remarked. "I made a little wager myself."

"Dinner's on me, Daniel!" Daphne waved him off as she and Margot went to the booths and the rest of the outbuildings.

"Remember, sound like a pro and use the number, not the name of the horse!" he called after her.

The crowd dispersed. Some people stayed near the rails, some went for refreshments; others left or just milled around to check out the grounds.

"Wow, I didn't expect that!" Daphne said.

Margot laughed. "Of course, you did."

"Okay, fine. But not like that."

"It doesn't matter. He meant it, and that's what counts."

"Yes, you're right. And I made money on a horse!"

The girls asked for their winnings in proper form and tucked the money away safely in their purses. It was quieter around the outbuildings than it had been right by the track and well shaded from the hot afternoon sun. They decided to take a little break and walk around. They came across offices, external stables and barns. There was still a fair amount of activity in some areas, people running in and out of the admin offices and horses being tended to at the barns. Between a deserted stable and a maintenance shed, there seemed to be something strange on the ground. Curious, the girls moved closer and saw it was a man's outstretched fist, fingers down in the mud, closed tightly.

CHAPTER SIXTEEN

"Is that..?" Daphne started.

"If you're going to say a fist, I think it is."

"We need to move closer." The girls stood there for a moment, wanting, but not wanting, to find out more. They looked around, but miraculously, with all the people at the track that day; there was no one nearby.

They moved closer to the lifeless arm, near enough to see to whom the extended hand belonged. They looked up the arm of the gray suit, followed it up to the crown of dark hair face down in the dirt. Daphne registered a guess first, recognizing the frame and suit. She gasped. "Efrem!"

They could not believe their eyes. In between a pair of buildings, was Efrem Goldberg, lying facedown in the mud. His arm was extended with a gash at the back of his head, bleeding profusely. His neck was turned slightly so that as they moved closer, they knew for sure the man's identity by his profile. Margot looked at his back and thought she saw it moving. "I think he's breathing." She started blaring out orders to Daphne who nodded and ran. "I'll stay here. Go get Tom and try to find a doctor or first aid attendant. Call an ambulance!"

Daphne stopped at the first building doorway and called for help. After a brief conversation with the man inside, she carried on, while he ordered the on-site ambulance to come and ran out to help Margot.

By the time Tom arrived, followed by plain clothed and uniformed officers, almost every member of the

Santa Lucia social set was in tow. The ambulance crew loaded their victim onto a stretcher. Rebecca, who was at the back of the crowd, was ushered forward as people recognized who was hurt. "Oh, Efrem," she wailed and almost fainted. Margot supported her as she regained her strength. Betty arrived shortly and stayed at her friend's side, while Margot observed all that was going on.

"Rebby, dear, what's going on?" A feeble older voice was coming from behind the group.

"Papa? What are you doing here? I didn't see you." Rebecca was startled to see her father here, of all places.

Isaac came over to comfort his daughter. "I came by for the races. Just a drive out, maybe get some lunch. What happened?"

"Oh, Papa. Efrem's been hurt. They don't know if he's going to wake up." She cried on Isaac's shoulder as he hushed her and smoothed her hair.

Tom briefly stopped the first aid crew, asking short questions. As it turned out, Efrem was alive, but unconscious. He had received a serious blow to the back of his head and was breathing, but his vital signs were not good and the crew wouldn't say any more. They needed to rush him to Santa Lucia General immediately.

"I found this in his hand, though." The attendant who'd spoken to Tom gave him something. Margot, who'd been close during the exchange, could not believe what she saw. It was a group of diamonds, which were fixed together, but looked like they'd been torn from a bigger strand, such as *the* missing necklace.

Her mouth dropped quickly as she caught Tom's eye. He kept his reaction in check and motioned for someone to bring an evidence bag into which he slipped the gems. Rebecca and Isaac saw it, too. She cried harder, while Isaac shook his head and uttered a firm, "Oy-vey!" and rolled his eyes to the heavens.

The ambulance crew insisted that they had to take the victim to the hospital or they could lose him. Tom gave the okay. Rebecca insisted on going with them in the Cadillac Eureka ambulance wagon with Isaac following behind.

The news about the gems in Efrem's fist made its rounds through the crowd, starting with the truth that he had in his hand a few stones that could possibly be from the real necklace that was missing, to a more embellished version that he'd ripped the necklace off of Miss Santa Lucia's neck and had been carrying around the diamonds all along. Being that the commotion had caused a longer break between races, a bigger crowd was forming.

"Margot, can I get a picture? You found the body, right?" Jake brought his camera up to his face and snapped away, not waiting for her reply.

Margot put her arm up to shield her eyes from the flash, while Loretta made her way to her. "Mar! What did you see? Did I hear right? Efrem's dead with the necklace in his hands?" Lenny trailed behind Loretta, writing down everything he heard and saw, furiously flipping through his notepad as he scribbled.

Margot shook her head, a little dazed from the flashes, the shock, everything that seemed to be happening at once and stepped aside, leaning out of the way against one of the buildings, not answering anything. She noticed Tom was busy with the crime scene and heard him curtly ordering commands, mentioning how that because the victim, or body, had to be moved it wasn't a clean scene. There could be tampering, missing evidence, conflicting clues everywhere and for them all to be very thorough, not to discount anything or anyone they found.

Loretta moved closer to Margot, eagerly waiting for her to answer and tell her everything she'd seen, pestering her with constant questions. It took a lot for Margot to snap, but when she did, it was memorable. "Loretta Simpson! You of all people! How could you forget? It was just about a month ago that you found Constance lying dead. Give me a minute, would you? How do you think I feel? Leave me alone!" In front of almost everyone they knew—their best Poppy Cove clientele, the unflappable Margot Williams lost her cool.

"I've been waiting to see that happen. Good for you, boss! Couldn't have happened at a better time," remarked Irene from the group. She was pushing her way forward with Eddie in tow. She glowered at Loretta. "You and your shutterbug, give her some room. If the police aren't hassling her, why are you?"

Daphne made her way to Margot's side, both of them surprised to see Irene after what she'd said yesterday and especially in the company of Eddie again. "What are you doing here? I thought you said you wouldn't be caught dead near this place." Daphne cringed when she realized her choice of words, given the circumstances.

"Eddie had to meet some people," Irene shrugged. "It was a day out for me." She was in blue denim capris and a sleeveless white blouse tied at the waist, obviously casually dressed and did not come from the VIP area. Eddie was in jeans and a t-shirt as well, looking a little ruffled with his greasy hair out of place and shirt untucked. He flinched when he saw Tom and kept trying to hide his right hand behind his back.

"I thought we told you not to come up here," Tom stated flatly. Eddie said nothing in return. He just continued to fidget as Tom noticed his actions. Tom walked over and grabbed his wrist. Eddie's palm was covered in a makeshift bandage of what seemed to be a cleaning rag. "What happened here, son?" Tom enquired. He pulled off the cloth and saw small cuts and swelling. "Looks like wood splinters. What have you been up to, Eddie?"

"Nothing." He whipped his hand back. "I ran into some associates, you know? Just talking and ran my hand along a new fence rail, that's all."

Tom continued to scrutinize Eddie. Eddie squirmed under his gaze, still not saying much, but shifting his posture in an agitated manner. Officer Riley, who was also in undercover garb, came up to Tom. "Malone, we might have our weapon here."

"Don't move, we're not done," Tom said to Eddie. "You neither," he indicated to Irene. His attention turned to Riley's find. A couple of other uniformed men, most likely locals, as Tom didn't recognize them, were standing around a two-by-four piece of lumber dropped on the ground just a few feet away. One end looked roughed up and stained with more than just mud. "Get this to the boys at the Santa Lucia crime lab." One of the uniformed men ran off to a squad car, getting a larger evidence bag, while another kept snapping photos of the area, including the wooden bar before it was removed. "Any idea where this came from?" Tom addressed the crowd, looking for answers from someone associated with the track.

A short, stocky man wearing a maintenance uniform stepped up. "Probably from over there, by that barn," he indicated with a jerk of his thumb. "We're adding on to that building. Making more stalls."

"Who had access to this?"

The man shrugged. "Well, anybody. It's all just there. The construction crew doesn't work on the weekends and the weather was going to be dry, so we just left it all out."

Tom zeroed in on Eddie again. "Been playing in the woodpile, Eddie?"

"Nah, look I told you, I was talking to some friends. I just rubbed my hand along a wood fence, that's all."

Tom grabbed him by his collar. "You're going in. Take him back to the Santa Lucia station. Her, too." He indicated Irene. "Separate cars."

Both Eddie and Irene were grabbed by their arms and ushered out under Tom's command. The tough girl's exterior was crumbling, indicating she thought she might be in real trouble. She gave a pleading look, making Margot forget all about their squabble. "I'll call your grandmother. She's stronger than you think. Don't worry," she called to Irene. Margot wasn't sure if that was necessarily true, but it's what the girl needed to hear at the time.

"Well, that's just great!" Mary Ann Rutherford was stomping around the crowd, crown and sash askew. "My first public appearance as queen and no one's watching."

"Calm down, Mary Ann. They said the presentation would go on, just a little later." Princess Caroline and Ralph were tagging behind her. "It's just a delay."

"Fine, but who's going to remember my debut? All they're going to think about is the guy lying in the mud!" She pouted.

Her mother, who was one of the appointed chaperones for the event, yarded off Mary Ann. "Now that's enough out of you! This is no way for Miss Santa Lucia or my daughter to behave," she hissed in a tone that she hoped was discreet, but everyone heard her loud and clear.

"Oh, get over yourself. Today's about the horse races, not us," Caroline chimed in. "You don't see the Dairy Queen acting this way," she added, indicating how the local reigning royalty was nowhere to be seen in the crime scene crowd. "She stayed in the stands, mingling and behaving herself. That's where we should be, too."

"Yes. Caroline's right, it's an excellent opportunity for you to show everyone how delightful you can be," Mrs. Rutherford added, taking charge. "Girls, let's go back to the stands and show Santa Ynez how friendly we are!"

The troupe left with Ralph straggling in tow, following behind, not sure where he should be. He wasn't exactly part of the court, but he knew if he weren't at the queen's beck and call, he'd hear about it later.

The rest of the Santa Lucians and others who'd gathered around the incident began to disperse, some returning to the stands, some leaving the grounds earlier than intended, unnerved due to the shocking events. All the while, Baroness von Eissen surveyed the happenings at a distance, nodding to her henchmen sons—not getting involved, but very interested all the same.

CHAPTER SEVENTEEN

It was business as usual the next morning when Daphne and Margot met up at the store. There was little time for anything else. They quickly glossed over how Lenny Cohen had the scoop on the racetrack events in the day's *Times*, which was a surprisingly faithful write-up to what they'd witnessed first hand. Being that Betty and Irene both had the day off and neither Margot nor Daphne had heard from either of them, they assumed there was no change in Efrem's condition or any further developments regarding Eddie's part in the affair.

As with every Monday, the store was closed, but the back room was humming with activity, as there was so much to do with the new holiday line. It was coming along nicely and Marjorie had it all was under control. The girls played with holiday window ideas and sorted out new lots of handbags, sparkly brooches and trinkets. With all the new arrivals, they decided to forget the town troubles for a little while and had a laugh playing dress up. One of their favorite new items was a crystal blue pin designed in a concentric fashion with one big stone in the middle and smaller ones radiating outward, forming a snowflake design. Margot paired it with one of the surplus wrap white silk blouses and a floor-length circular skirt in shot taffeta, the same clear hue as the gems. The effect was stunning on the mannequin. They put the display near a glass case filled with other new and dazzling pieces. Then, they spent the rest of the morning going over store business and what direction they wanted to take for spring, bandying about ideas that went from floral gardens to the new mod art atomic prints, which would certainly be different from past collections and might cause some of paying clients such as Nancy Lewis to react dramatically.

When one o'clock rolled around, the girls went for lunch at the Poppy Lane Tearoom across the street. Lana brought them coffee and took their orders for soup and sandwiches as she sat them at a recently vacated table by a window. With a morning of work behind them and no news regarding the recent events, Margot asked her friend how her evening had gone after they had dropped her off.

Daphne was quiet for a moment, took a sip of her coffee and blushed. "Fine," was all she said, but the big grin on her face betrayed her attempt at playing it cool.

Margot smirked. "Just fine, huh?"

Daphne couldn't stop smiling. "It was nice. After we left you, we strolled on the beach."

"And?"

"It was nice," she repeated. In all of the time that they'd known each other, Margot had never known Daphne to be so coy. She appeared truly smitten, and it didn't seem like it was fleeting. Their lunches arrived and Daphne took a bite of her tuna salad sandwich and changed the subject. "Did Tom come by last night?"

"No." Margot blew on her hot tomato soup before sipping it. "I haven't heard from him since we left the track."

"You mean, the crime scene," Daphne inferred. She gave a little shiver. "No word from anyone yet. Everyone's really quiet. There doesn't even seem to be good gossip floating around here. Wonder what's going on?"

Margot shrugged noncommittally as the two continued their lunch in companionable silence. Before

174 *Death of a Beauty Queen*

long, it was interrupted with the whirlwind known as Loretta. "Okay, ladies, the pages are on the presses so I can tell you!"

The reporter sat down, clearing space for herself, almost elbowing soup in one friend's lap and sandwich in the other's. Those jewels? They were fake, too!"

"What?" Daphne asked as she set down her sandwich.

"I know! Can you believe it?" All conversation stopped in the café as the other diners looked in their direction. Loretta responded back a bit quieter. She didn't mind telling her two best friends a scoop, but the rest of Santa Lucia had to buy a paper to get the news. "The rocks found in Efrem's hand? They were just rock crystal, a new kind that almost fooled the police experts. Pretty good copies, but not real diamonds either."

The girls were puzzled. "So what exactly did he have in his hand? Was it the missing necklace, or another piece altogether?" Daphne asked.

"And why was he attacked?" followed up Margot.

"The police have a few ideas they're looking into. Efrem had surgery last night to alleviate the pressure on his skull and stitch up the wound, but he's still critical and hasn't woken up yet. The police are keeping an eye on the room. It's a bit of a zoo with doctors, nurses and who knows what medical experts looking him over all the time."

"How about Isaac? Does he have any answers about the necklaces?"

Loretta shrugged. "He's been at Rebecca's side since Efrem was found, just fretting and fussing. The police are keeping an eye on Efrem's room and speaking to Isaac while they wait, but no dice. He seems to know nothing and just keeps futzing over his daughter and son in law."

Margot thought about another aspect of that day. "What about Irene and Eddie? Any news about them?"

"Irene was actually pretty co-operative. Turns out the latest events scared her and she was polite to the police, answered all of their questions. If Eddie was up to no good, she didn't have any part in it. They let her go with her grandmother, who turns out to have a son who's Irene's uncle, who's some highfaluting lawyer and willing to represent her if necessary.

"This has been quite the scoop for our young rookie. Lenny's crowing around like head rooster. Weathers's sitting around, all mopey. He went into the editor's office, whining and complaining that he should have covered it under the police beat, but Lenny was on the ball. He got the pictures from Jake and turned his angle from the race focus and got two major headlines. Talk about Golden Boy!" Loretta grinned. Her personal feelings about Michael Weathers were still on the fence. He could write a good crime tale, but when he had subbed for her Society Page briefly, he ruffled the feathers of the social set that she was still trying to calm down. She ordered a cup of coffee, obviously settling in.

As she sipped, she continued to recount what she could about the week's events. "It's all really murky. I mean, all of Nora's murder suspects were there yesterday and were seen around the track, according to what Lenny figured out." She pushed her cat-eye glasses up her nose and began listing the details on her fingertips. "Although Efrem was conked out and left for dead, he did have what everyone thought might be the missing necklace, so he's not out of the woods for Nora's murder, and the rest of the piece—even if it is fake—is still missing. We also don't know where the real diamonds are. I don't have any answers about that. As for the murder, one theory is that Efrem did kill

Nora and someone yesterday was out to avenge her death. More likely, as an off-the-record junior policeman spilled to Lenny, it's the same person who killed Nora and it now seems that their motive was the necklace all along."

She took another sip and continued. "We know about Eddie being taken in and his damaged hand." Her audience of two nodded in response. "Then, Ralph and Mary Ann aren't exactly in the clear either, and Dirk kept disappearing throughout the afternoon. We all thought he was just refilling his flask, and maybe he was, but a track employee swears he saw him in that area around the barns just before Efrem was found." Loretta sat back, proud of her surmising skills. In a flash, Loretta sat straighter, grabbed her notebook, scribbling furiously, then looked up. "What if it was someone else?"

Margot considered her question. "What do you mean?"

"Well, what about someone from the ball, wanting the necklace. I'm sure you two were too busy that night with the dresses, but there were a lot of coveting eyes on the piece, like the Baroness Eva von Eissen, Nancy Lewis, even Elaine Stinson."

"Now, come on," Margot scoffed. "Could you really see any of those women breaking into the Burbank's and committing murder over a necklace?"

"No, I guess not." Loretta agreed it was a stretch. She hesitated, licked her lips nervously and reached out to Margot's arm. "Listen, Mar, I'm really sorry about yesterday."

Margot sat back with a light frown on her face and then remembered her outburst from yesterday. In all of the news and happenings, she'd forgotten her anger. "Don't worry about it, Loretta." She patted her friend's arm.

"No, I mean it. In all the excitement, I didn't think about what you'd seen, just reporting the story. Sometimes my nose for news gets the better of me."

At the time, Margot was upset, but after all that had happened, she had let it go as well. "It was just a shocking moment, with so much going on. It's fine."

Loretta smiled, gave a sigh of relief and withdrew her hand.

Margot nodded and like her friends, digested the news and their lunch in relative quiet. "So," she concluded, "we're nowhere, still."

"Not quite," Loretta grinned. "We know that Daniel loves Daphne!"

Daphne blushed and her companions smirked. "Well yes," she demurred, out of character.

Loretta nudged her friend. "Hey, that's good news, right?"

Daphne scrunched up her nose. "By the way, how did you hear about that? You weren't there when he said it."

"Oh!" Loretta gave a little wave. "Darling, it's common knowledge! Everyone heard. He was very enthusiastic about it."

Even though Daphne pretended to be mortified, anyone with eyes could see she was pleased and broke into a smile. Her love fog was cleared briskly as she looked over towards the front door of Poppy Cove, where a black-garbed silhouette was looming. "Is that the Baroness rattling our door?"

Margot followed her gaze. "Wonder what she's doing there? We have an appointment set for tomorrow afternoon." She left her companions at the Tearoom and went to meet Eva. "Hello, Baroness. What brings you to the store today?"

"Well," she huffed. "Our appointment. Two o'clock, on the 7th of October."

"Sorry, but our appointment is for tomorrow, Tuesday, the 8th."

"No, it's not."

Margot hesitated, knowing it wasn't the best form to tick off a client, especially a new one who was royalty and could bring in good orders to the shop if they could find something suitable for her new look. Trouble was, Margot hadn't given much thought to the Baroness and her wardrobe, as she was going to use this afternoon to focus on that very matter. She noticed Eva had a Poppy Cove business card in her hand and asked to see it. Written in Margot's own clear and legible handwriting was tomorrow's date. She politely pointed it out to Eva.

"It doesn't matter. I'm here now; you will see me," she firmly stated, not budging, waiting for Margot to unlock the door.

Margot gave a heavy sigh and thought she might as well go through with it, doubting she'd be any better prepared tomorrow for such a difficult and demanding client. She sat the woman down in the salon and excused herself to get her sketchbook, any notes she had, and pulled a surprised Marjorie from her work at the back to give her a hand.

The appointment went as expected. Anything Margot would suggest, the Baroness disagreed with, always reverting back to the heavy black wools and thicker silks, completely out of place for the local climate and contemporary fashions. Marjorie interjected where she could, doing her best to try to win the potential client over. After fifteen minutes, it was clear that they'd reached an impasse, and Margot had to admit defeat. "Eva, as much as it pains me to say, I do think your desires may be achieved elsewhere. Perhaps Martin's Department Store may be able to cater to your needs. They have a wider range of suppliers and may be able to help you better."

The Baroness sized up the designer and dressmaker. "Yes. Maybe you're right. I have my ways and perhaps a more established trade would be able to fulfill my requirements."

Daphne came in as the Baroness was rising to leave, sensing the tension in the room. Eva gave the store and its occupants a final gaze as she left. "This Santa Lucia, it's a very provincial and little place. You know nothing of European ways and society. Even your royalty are impostors, just like what you call diamonds." She turned on her heels, closing the front door with a slam.

"Wow," Daphne remarked. "So that's how that went."

Margot didn't know whether to laugh or cry. On occasion, she'd lost a customer or two, as she had learned you can't please everyone all the time while staying true to yourself, but this one had been exhausting.

Marjorie sat down in a heap and remarked, "Dear, you're better off without her. She would've never been happy. Your work and your clients are much better than that. Let Martin's handle the likes of her!"

Margot recapped the scene to Daphne. After a brief commiseration and eventual laugh, everyone got back to work. Thankfully, the day progressed smoothly. Just as the girls were getting ready to leave at five, the telephone rang. Daphne answered the call, becoming very animated during the conversation. She clicked the receiver down in an excited manner.

"Who was that?" Margot asked.

"Mother. Grace is in labor and they're all going down to the hospital!"

"Who's all?"

"Both my parents, William, Lizzie, too. Everyone's all excited! I've got to go!"

"Of course. How's she doing?"

"Fine, they say. The contractions started yesterday, but she and William didn't say anything until they were closer together. The doctor sent her to the hospital, so it shouldn't be too long now, but you never know." Daphne was all aflutter looking for her keys, sweater and handbag, all items that she already had in her possession.

Margot took the keys out of her friend's hand and settled her down a little. "Why don't I drive your car for you? I'll drop you off at the hospital and bring your car back here. I'm sure you can get a ride home with your family and pick up the car from here later tonight or tomorrow."

"Uh, yes, sure." She looked around distractedly. "My purse?"

Margot laughed. "In your other hand! Come on, let's go. I'll get you there safely."

CHAPTER EIGHTEEN

The Santa Lucia General Hospital Maternity Ward waiting room was full of Huntington-Smythes, among other expectant families. Being that Grace's family was from Denver, Colorado, and had just been notified that she was in labor, her parents were on their way, but not in attendance yet. When Daphne and Margot arrived, Patricia was perched on the edge of her seat, waiting happily but impatiently for her first grandchild. Gerald, equally anticipating the arrival, kept in rhythm with his son, the father to be, pacing and chain smoking. Lizzie sat in a corner, socks slouched, knees not as close together as they should be, with her face hidden behind a *True Detective* magazine, chewing and popping her gum loudly. She was also taking puffs off a stolen cigarette and generally avoiding the entire scene.

Daphne greeted her family with hugs and got the scoop on her sister-in-law. Grace's labor pains were getting closer together. In a short time, the doctors would give her a little something to help her relax and make it much more pleasant to give birth. All the family could do was sit and wait.

As Margot was leaving the hospital, she ran into a familiar face that was looking worn out. "Betty, any news about Efrem?"

"No, no change yet. I've been here all day with Rebecca. She's been here since they brought him in last night," Betty sighed, and then looked at her employer. "What are you doing here?"

Margot beamed, happy to share some good news. "Daphne's sister-in-law Grace has gone into labor. Her whole family is here. Her mother called the shop and Daphne was too excited to drive herself, so I brought her over. I thought it might be nice to be a part of some good news for a change, after all that's been happening."

Betty smiled for the first time that day. "Oh, how nice! How is she? Anything to report yet?"

"No, nothing. They're all just pacing and waiting," Margot replied. There was an awkward pause in the conversation, as she knew Betty was preoccupied with the state of her friend. "I'm sorry to hear there's no progress in Efrem's condition. Rebecca must be so worried."

Betty nodded. "I've been trying to get her to step out, even to the cafeteria, or just outside to get a breath of air, but she won't. Isaac couldn't pull her away. She finally sent him home about an hour ago. He was looking pretty tired himself, constantly fretting and fussing. Honestly, I don't know if he helped or made her more worried."

Margot sympathetically smiled at her friend and employee, innocently offering, "Is there anything I can do?"

Betty's eyes went wide. "Oh, do you mean it?"

Margot felt a slight twinge in her stomach, not sure if she'd volunteered to do more than she wanted to. "Sure," she finally said, sensing Betty's desperation.

"Thanks. Come sit with Efrem."

"What?"

"Just for a few minutes, not long. I want to get Rebecca to stretch her legs, and maybe eat something. We won't be long, I promise," she assured her boss.

"But I don't really know him," Margot replied.

"Sure you do! Really, we won't be long and all he's doing is sleeping. Rebecca won't leave him or go out on her own. If I tell her you'll stay with him, she'll be okay with that. Besides, there's a police officer stationed right outside the door. If Efrem does happen to wake up, just use the buzzer by the bed and the nurses will come. They'll also get Rebecca." Betty noticed the look on Margot's face and matched it with her own pleading glance. An expectant silence followed.

Margot didn't know what to do. She had wanted to go home after such a trying day and thought about asking Daphne if she'd do it, but she didn't want to take her away from her family. It certainly was awkward, but she couldn't give Betty a good enough reason not to do it, other than being nervous about being in the same room with a man in a coma who may or may not be trustworthy. Then again, Betty had no doubt of his innocence and they were in a hospital, with a cop in the hallway and the nurse's station only a bell ring away. Chances are he wouldn't wake up while she was there anyway. Finally she agreed to do it.

"Thank you so much, Margot! She really needs a break." Betty grabbed her arm and hurried her along. Margot could barely keep steady in her heels on the highly polished and sterilized floors. "Just wait here; I'll go speak to her," Betty remarked as they skidded to a stop outside a private room marked 'Goldberg.'

Stationed by the room to the left of the door was a young rookie officer sitting in a rather uncomfortable wooden chair. He looked vaguely familiar to Margot. She recognized him from her visits to the station to see Tom. She smiled and nodded, which he returned. She could hear the whirrs and beeps coming from Efrem's darkened room. The only illumination came from the monitors and a small bedside lamp on low. After a few

184 *Death of a Beauty Queen*

long moments, Rebecca came to the doorframe, reluctantly agreeing to leave Efrem's side for just a few minutes. The poor girl was exhausted—limp-haired and wearing the same dress she'd worn since yesterday. She looked wrinkled and weak on her friend's arm. Rebecca thanked Margot and promised her she'd be right back. She gave another glance towards her husband, lying motionless, as Betty dragged her out of the dark into the brightly lit hallway.

Margot took a deep breath, went into the room, and did what she'd agreed to do. It was creepily quiet with only the sounds of hospital machines and even, slow breaths from Efrem. He looked deathly white, paler than the pastel green sheets, with the back half of his head wrapped in thick swaddling gauze. She sat on the chair beside him, still warm from Rebecca. She watched him for a few minutes, not really knowing what to do. Generally, Margot was a self-assured confident woman, but sitting there in the stillness with someone who was just an acquaintance and barely there himself made her feel uneasy. She didn't know him well enough to touch him or take his hand. *What if he did wake up?* she thought. Immediately, her eyes zeroed in on the call buzzer that was clearly marked, and it gave her a small sense of relief. Would he know or remember who she was? *Anyway, Betty and Rebecca probably wouldn't be long,* she rationalized, *and chances are nothing will happen.*

She jumped in her seat when she heard the creak of a wooden chair. The rookie outside the door had shifted his position. Margot relaxed again, then felt antsy. Nothing was happening and there was no sign of Rebecca and Betty returning. *What would it hurt,* she figured, *to go talk to the cop at the door, to someone?* She'd still keep her word to Rebecca and stay near

Efrem, sure to be alert if he woke up or if something changed, but this made her feel awkward.

She got up, stood in the doorway, with her back to Efrem. The officer, who turned out to be Laurence Franklin, was in his first year as a Santa Lucia Police Officer. He was a polite young man, maybe a year or two younger than she was, and worked often on cases with Tom. Margot felt more relaxed while she waited for the ladies to return and almost forgot why she was there. Then she heard a shuffle from behind. She turned in what felt like slow motion, glanced toward the wardrobe at the right of the room and found it peculiar that it was now wide open. Then she saw a figure dressed head to toe in light green surgical garb. The form encompassed the top of Efrem's hospital bed. It took a split second for her to register what was happening. "Oh, my God!" she exclaimed when she could comprehend what she was witnessing.

Margot's gasp alerted the docile officer out of his chair so fast that it fell over in the hallway. He jumped up with his hand on his gun, pushing Margot to the side in the doorframe. She stepped back, allowing Franklin to step in. "Freeze! Police!" he yelled dramatically, trying to muster up all the power in his voice, but coming across unsure and shaky, his youth and inexperience betraying him.

The figure was trying to smother Efrem with a pillow. It was all dressed in a hospital uniform, including a surgical mask, cap and shoe covers. It hid all the person's features, other than the fact that the person was short. The figure stopped, dropped the pillow and turned, barreled past the officer, knocking him over, then tripping Margot on his way in the hall. She lost her footing on the slippery polished linoleum and felt her heels give way painfully. The next thing she knew, she was on the floor, her right ankle in a funny position, and watching the figure go out an emergency exit at the end of the hall. Franklin was in hot pursuit. He gave Margot a quick glance, called for someone to help her, and took off after the assailant. She continued to yell for help after she realized she couldn't stand up. There was something seriously wrong with her leg—come to think of it, both of them. As a couple of nurses and a doctor came to attend to her and Efrem, she surrendered to the pain.

CHAPTER NINETEEN

"I knew I shouldn't have left him; I just shouldn't have," Rebecca lamented. Efrem's room was now crawling with medical staff and police, and the ladies had been ordered out of the room until further notice. The cops and nurses were at odds, the first wanting to investigate what had happened, and the latter wanting to check the condition of the patient. There was constant discreet snapping, both sides issuing commands not to harm or touch anything, for fear of worsening either Efrem's state or hindering the collection of clues. Rebecca shook herself and remembered to ask, "How's Margot?"

Betty was sitting in the ward lounge, holding her distraught friend's hand, guiltily fretting over the whole situation. They'd only been gone five minutes to the cafeteria when there had been a flurry of activity. Then they were alerted that something had happened in Efrem's room. By time they got back, staff were loading Margot onto a gurney, and others were dealing with bells and buzzers coming from Efrem's room.

"The doctor says she has a broken ankle. It's a bad break in two places, and her left one is strained as well. He's set a cast on it and decided to admit her just in case shock sets in. They have her under police protection in the event that the attacker comes back. When she's ready, the cops also want to question her to see if she knows who knocked her down."

"And tried to kill Efrem again," Rebecca finished the statement. She sighed, anxious to hear about the state of her husband.

"I'm going to call Dwight and let him know I won't be home. Do you want me to call your father and have him come back?" Betty offered.

"Yes, please. And Betty, thanks for everything. You've been a good friend. Once Dad arrives, why don't you go home to your husband?" Rebecca was trembling, nervously about to cry, but doing her best to put on a good face.

"Are you sure?" Betty was relieved, but didn't want to show it. She'd been there all day and she really wanted to go home.

"Yes, it's what I would want to do," Rebecca replied sadly.

"Well, we'll see." Betty also wanted to check in on her employer, to see if there was anything, anything at all she could do. She went to the bank of pay phones near the coffee and cigarette machines. She talked briefly with Dwight, relieved to hear her husband's voice. He was kind and supportive, but hungry and wasn't sure what to eat as she always had dinner on the table for him. She laughed to herself and told him there was luncheon meat in the refrigerator, along with bread and cheese, so he should just make himself a sandwich and she'd be home when she could. Isaac was not so easy to reach. She tried the home number that Rebecca had given her and then looked up Mendelson's Jewelers in the phone book. There was no answer there, either. By the time she got back to Rebecca, there was a nurse and doctor speaking with her friend.

"So according to the tests, your husband was not harmed in the attack," stated the doctor, looking at his chart and reporting his findings. Even in such a terrible situation, Betty couldn't help but notice he was rather attractive in a smart sort of way, with his dark-rimmed glasses and well behaved hair, set off by the white lab coat and stethoscope. She blushed a little as she smiled and then corrected her thoughts by thinking of her Dwight instead. The doctor continued. "In fact, we've seen a little more brain activity according to the charts, so it may have stimulated him into a waking state."

Rebecca's face lit up, but the doctor cautioned her. "It's not certain, so don't read too much into it. It's still a matter of waiting until he's ready to wake up."

"Can I go to him, doctor?"

"Yes, I think so. Just be prepared that you may not notice any change. Not yet, anyway."

Betty glanced down the hall and saw uniformed officers milling about, noticing Detective Riley was there, but not Tom. "Are the police done in his room?"

The doctor nodded. "I asked them to be brief and consider the patient's condition. They also mentioned that they want to speak with each of you individually, to see if you saw or heard anything. It appears that someone had been hiding in the wardrobe closet, waiting for an opportunity to strike. Think about that and let them know if you remember seeing anything." He walked away briskly, off to deal with another situation, with a nurse following in tow.

The women looked at each other, shocked. They could swear that the whole time Efrem had not been left unattended, so how could anyone have slipped into the room unnoticed? Could that really have happened? Would it have happened all in that brief time that Margot was there? Then again, there were nurses, doctors and orderlies of all kinds who'd been coming in and out of the room, right past the police, too.

Riley spoke with Rebecca first, asking her if she remembered seeing anyone specifically hovering around the wardrobe in the room, acting differently, or doing anything she would question in respect to Efrem's care. She thought about it carefully, but nothing came to mind. Betty couldn't recall anything either. The theory that the police had surmised was that someone who was wearing hospital attire had slipped into the wardrobe about an hour before the attack and waited until Efrem was not directly being watched. Margot had left his side, with her back to him very briefly, but that was enough time for the person to act. They fled on foot, and from what Riley could report to the women, were still being pursued by the police.

Rebecca settled in at her husband's side, determined not to leave it until he woke up. Betty joined her after talking to Riley, making sure her friend was as comfortable as she could be. The whole time Efrem slept on and on. Betty eyed the room, looking at the wardrobe. It was in a dark corner, and large—the size of a walk-in closet. Someone could easily have slipped in there when no one was looking and, with the door slightly ajar, watch the room. They could wait in relative ease and silence. She shook her head trying to recall any possible memories of seeing anything like that happening and remembered nothing.

"Have you seen Margot yet?" Rebecca asked. Her tone of voice was flat and Betty couldn't read into it if she was upset with Margot.

"No," she answered with hesitation. "I was thinking of going to see her after you got settled in again."

Rebecca took Efrem's hand, thought, and nodded. After a few moments, she said, "Let her know I asked about her. And, well, tell her not to blame herself. It could have happened on my watch, too. I was starting to nod off myself. I just don't know how it all happened, that's all."

Betty patted her friend and turned to go. Rebecca had one more question. "Do you know when my father's coming?"

"I don't know; I couldn't get a hold of him."

"Oh," Rebecca said. "Well, maybe he took one of his sleeping pills. He still had some left from a prescription he got when he was coping with mother's death."

"Do you want me to stay?" Betty knew what she wanted the answer to be, but being ever the loyal friend, was prepared to remain at Rebecca's side.

"No, you go. I'll get one of the nurses to try to ring Dad in the morning if there's no change. My place is here by my husband, and I intend to stay here." She straightened up with a second wind bringing on a refreshed wifely stoicism.

Betty left her friend to make a quick stop to see Margot before going home to find what kind of mess her husband had left in the kitchen. Dwight was all thumbs when it came to cooking, but, honestly, how much damage could one man do by just making a sandwich?

Margot had been given her own private room. Her broken ankle was plastered from the start of her toes to just below the knee and was suspended in a cloth sling. Her left foot, which was mildly banged up, was taped and under the covers. She was in a hospital gown, sitting up in bed, with Daphne making a fuss with the pillows on her left side and Tom sitting to her right, holding her hand and talking quietly. Betty made her presence known by a light rap on the open door.

Margot smiled through her medicated haze and welcomed her. "Come on in, Betty; join the party!"

Daphne smirked. "Don't mind her; they have her on some pretty heavy painkillers. She did a real number on the broken one."

Betty gasped. "Oh, no! Did they have to operate?"

"No, it'll heal up perfectly, but she won't be in heels for a while," Daphne remarked.

Betty addressed the patient. "I feel just horrible, Margot. If I hadn't asked you to sit with Efrem, none of this would have happened."

"Ah, Betty, honey, don't worry about it," Margot slurred as she slapped the air. Betty had no idea when or if Margot had ever called her 'honey.'

"Betty, any idea when or how the attacker got into Efrem's room?" Tom was still on duty, just taking a short break to check on his girlfriend. "We talked with Margot before the medication kicked in. She didn't see anything, other than the open door on the wardrobe and the person standing at the top of the bed trying to smother Efrem, then fleeing when they were caught."

Betty shook her head. "I talked to your partner just a few minutes ago. I don't remember anything out of the ordinary."

Tom nodded. "Neither did Mar. No distinguishing sights, sounds, movements, scents, anything different that would signify another presence in the room?"

Again, Betty shook her head. Tom gently let go of his girlfriend's hand. She was dozing off, which was the best thing for her. A uniformed officer appeared at the door, signaling to him. He kissed Margot's forehead as he got up. "I've got to see to the case. We have someone keeping watch on her room too, now that she's possibly witnessed something that could be related to the case and could be in danger herself. Ladies," Tom acknowledged them as he left.

Betty suddenly remembered why Daphne was there. "Grace! How's she doing? Is the baby born yet?"

"No, we're all just waiting. I heard all the commotion with the police arriving and followed the trail to see what was going on. Imagine my surprise!"

"I know; it's just terrible isn't it?" They filled each other in about what they knew of the events and sat conspiring quietly at the now sleeping Margot's bedside.

"Ahem." A stern, older nurse came in the room to read Margot's chart. "The patient should have some rest now. She'll be fine. It's best if you take your conversation elsewhere."

Daphne and Betty left the room, but not before checking the washroom and closet doors. They saw that Jenkins was stationed outside, relieved that it was an experienced officer that they knew keeping an eye on their friend. The next day was Tuesday, and normally Betty's day off, but it was clear that Margot was going to be out of commission for a while. Also, Irene could possibly be tied up if Eddie was still a suspect and depending on the new arrival, it could be a long night for Daphne, too. She asked Betty to come in to work tomorrow, to which she agreed, saying it was the least she could do and they parted for the night.

Around nine p.m., the world was a different place. David Gerald Huntington-Smythe (named after his two grandfathers) had made his way into the world, a healthy eight pounds, four ounces, with all his fingers and toes perfectly pink, his mother resting and doing just fine. The police had found hospital scrubs thrown in a nearby bush, most likely from the attempted murderer and were scanning the area for clues, as well as analyzing the clothes at the station's lab. Efrem had decided to rejoin the world of the living as well, just before David's debut. The injured man fluttered his eyes, muttering, "I, I, I..." before smiling at his Rebecca and drifting into a normal sleep state as she buzzed the nurses' station. The hospital staff assured her that he was basically out of the woods and just needed to rest.

Relieved, she wondered what he was trying to say. *I? I love you, I'm sorry, I didn't do it, I'm innocent, I did do it?* Rebecca was driving herself crazy with a new set of worries. Then, just as she was wondering where her father was, he came into the room and sat down beside her, fatigued.

In Margot's drugged slumber, she kept picturing in her dreams what had happened. The events were out of order and odd. She dreamt she was outside, with diamonds in her hands, then she was the one in a hospital bed with a pillow coming towards her face; she was chasing someone; she was the one being chased. The only constant in the images was that there was a man, she was sure of it in the green uniform, an older man, with watery eyes. Becoming clearer was the image of wisps of gray hair peeking out from behind the cap. That was getting stronger and stronger. It was so strong that the vision woke her with a painful start. Her eyes flew open and she knew who the attacker was. She was shocked but she knew she was right, just sorry to be the one to tell the news. She buzzed for a nurse and called out loud which sent Jenkins running in and ordered him to immediately call Tom. She knew who had run her down, but wasn't sure why.

Rebecca woke up with her head resting on her father's shoulder. She was relieved to see that Efrem was gaining a healthier complexion and felt calm for the first time since the incident at the track. The peace was short lived as Tom tapped Isaac on the shoulder, telling him quietly to come along with him and Jenkins down to the station. He sighed, nodded and slumped in defeat, knowing his deceit was over. Rebecca became fully awake and wide-eyed, grasping her father's arm with a bewildered look on her face. "What's going on, Papa?"

He got up without a fuss, gently removing her arm. "Rebby, I have to go." Rebecca started to get up but he gently held her down. "I am done, thank God in heaven, it is over. Look after your husband. He is a good man." He started trembling. "I'm sorry, sorry. I have been so bad, I do not deserve you. If you can find it in your heart, please forgive me. I have been lost." He aged about ten years as he volunteered himself to the law.

As she watched him go, Efrem stirred. Rebecca turned back in her seat to see her husband alert. She wept in joy and confusion, not sure which was the stronger emotion. She gently stroked his cheek as he kept coming back to her. He repeated from earlier, "I, I…"

"Yes, darling, take your time. I love you, too."

He shook his head. "I, Isaac. Isaac, c-c-catch him. He's, he's up to no good." He gasped and then fell back into a light slumber, peaceful that he'd said what he needed to say. There was no other way he could break it. He knew what was going on and he had to let people know, no matter who heard it or how it came about.

Rebecca sat back; shocked further, reeling, alone and bereft that her father was taken away and her husband had retreated back into his own world. She didn't understand what it all amounted to, but she somehow knew it was all adding up to something wrong and her father was in way over his head. No one could comfort her now.

CHAPTER TWENTY

The news of the sordid tale spread like wildfire through Santa Lucia. Isaac Abraham Mendelson had been a desperate man with a tortured soul. With Rabbi Hertzfeld at his side instead of a lawyer, he confessed his whole sordid misadventure to the police. Being that he gave a full confession and was willing to take whatever punishment the law deemed appropriate, he told all he knew and the details made their way to the public at rocket speed through the *Times* and from idle but unbelievably accurate gossip.

It all started when his wife of 33 years, Miriam, had passed away from cancer, leaving a grief-stricken Isaac with insurmountable hospital bills. Adding to his financial woes was the fact that Martin's Department Store had introduced their own fine jewelry and watch repair department, which took a cut of his business. Having Efrem come on board with new ideas and fresh eyes helped, but not in the amounts Isaac needed to keep from losing his shirt. He was too proud to tell anyone of his money troubles, including his family and his religious community, even though they all would have done their best to help and support him.

Isaac had always played a little at the track, nothing serious, but a few dollars here and there. Being a widower on his own, gave him more time to think of his growing problems. He started going to the track and betting more often, sometimes hitting a substantial winning streak. Instead of using the money to pay down his bills, he took bigger and bigger risks on long shots and higher odds, briskly losing even more money than he had, all the while keeping the information away from those who loved him in his shame.

There was, however, someone who saw his plight. Skulking around the track were the von Eissen brothers, Alex and Walter, sons of the mysterious Baroness Eva. The boys preyed on the weak, appearing generous and reasonable with quick cash loans to those in need. Isaac took them up on their offers, using more money to gamble and losing even greater amounts, which the boys did not take too kindly.

Isaac soon found out that they were part of a bigger crime syndicate that ran all kinds of games and schemes. Being that he was a jeweler by trade, Isaac was given a task under their umbrella that suited the von Eissens' interests to a *t*. Alex and Walter told him that they would forgive his debts and pay him handsomely if he helped them out every now and then with a little work. If he didn't agree to do it, they could take him and his business down within a week.

Isaac felt he had no choice but to go along with their proposal. Every few weeks at the synagogue after morning prayer, the boys would slip him a black velvet bag containing fake manufactured diamonds that they would have him work into jewelry—necklaces, rings, brooches, earrings. They would demand a deadline and pick up a finished piece, bringing more stones to him for a new exchange. The pieces would then be sold for a fortune through legitimate brokers as real diamond jewelry from Europe in larger centers—Los Angeles, New York, Chicago, Miami and the like. Once he did enough work that the von Eissen brothers felt had paid off his debt, they would talk about giving him a cut in cash. They never discussed the terms in detail. They told him that they would let him know when the score was settled. Isaac doubted that it would ever happen.

The rocks were good, sometimes even confusing Isaac for real stones as he worked on them. He told nobody what he was up to. He usually worked on the pieces either at home or late at night in the shop when Efrem wasn't around. Unfortunately, one day Efrem had forgotten his wallet at the shop and was amazed at the spectacular necklace Isaac was constructing. It was much grander than their usual work they did for custom or regular shop trinkets and Efrem became excited at the idea of them doing more pieces in this style. Isaac was irritated and tried to discourage him, telling him it was a special custom piece for someone out of town and it wasn't something Mendelson's Jewelers would do on a regular basis. The truth was, it was going to be the last piece he would do for the von Eissens. He wanted out. He'd been doing this for a few months now, since the late spring, and felt his debt was paid, no matter what they said. If they didn't agree, he was going to turn them in. He was done.

Isaac hoped that by working on the last fence piece in the evenings when Efrem was gone, his son-in-law would put it out of his mind. Unfortunately, that was not the case. Efrem couldn't get the design out of his thoughts—it was one of the most beautiful necklaces he'd seen in his life, surpassing any of the lovely but benign trinkets that were the usual shop fare for Santa Lucia. As Isaac worked late into the night, he took the mornings off from Mendelson's on occasion, using the excuse that he was pulling back from the store to give Efrem a chance to take over more of the shop business. All the while that Efrem was left alone, he pulled out Isaac's masterpiece and copied it as the gift token for the reigning Miss Santa Lucia, Nora Burbank.

Efrem sincerely thought that having the grand gems in the Charity Ball Fashion Show was a smart bold move to show the Santa Lucia social set what

Mendelson's Jewelers could be under his guidance. Innocently, he took Isaac's reticence as modesty, not that he had done anything wrong with creating it. Sure, he knew that the 'original' necklace was going to a private anonymous customer, but that didn't mean it couldn't be shown off if it was returned safely.

In the cold light of day on that fateful Monday morning after the fashion show, Efrem noticed a few things as he took the necklace out of the safe. He had been so focused on getting his copy made secretively and in a hurry; he never saw that a couple of the stones had a slightly different luster to them. The stones in Isaac's necklace looked so good and he never suspected that his father-in-law would ever use anything but the best diamonds. He didn't bother to pay much attention to the original, other than to make his own replica perfect. The closer he looked at the piece from the black velvet case he had in the safe on the Monday after the show, the more panicked and dry mouthed he became, as he noticed more detail. He convinced himself that the two pieces must have been switched backstage, with Nora now having Isaac's work and the replica he had made in the safe that morning. Out of his head with worry, he ran over to Poppy Cove to arrange for the switch.

In the meantime, Isaac had come into work, and noticed Efrem's agitated state throughout the day. Isaac went to the safe, saw that his work was there and continued on with the cleaning and watch repair orders that filled his Monday. All the while, he kept an eye on Efrem, knowing something was up. Later in the day when Efrem called Poppy Cove, Isaac listened intently. Having never bothered with the society pages in the *Santa Lucia Times*, Isaac hadn't seen the photos of Nora wearing the necklace. He had also spent his day tinkering in the back of the store, so it was the first he had heard of the necklace being used in the fashion show. He was fuming and anxious as he realized what Efrem had done behind his back.

Both men stayed in the store until closing time, nervy and touchy, staying out of each other's way. Fortunately, Mendelson's was busy with interest and requests after the fashion show. Isaac stayed in the back and let Efrem handle things, listening the entire time. As the day wore on, he was of mixed feelings and thoughts, secretly proud that the necklace garnered so much attention and that his son-in-law had taken the risk. However, the gnawing, worrying nature so ingrained in his old soul pre-occupied him with thoughts of how all of this was going to turn out. He couldn't tell anyone what he'd done; especially Efrem and, heaven forbid, his Rebby. As Efrem was busy, Isaac had another look at the necklace in the safe and, in his panic; he was no longer sure which one he had in the store—the von Eissen one or Efrem's re-creation. All he knew was that he needed to see the two side by side to compare them, and he couldn't wait until the next day.

He knew that breaking into the Burbank's was wrong, but if he could just slip in, he could get the necklace and compare the two at the shop. He might even be able to go into the house again and replace it without anyone knowing the difference. He could then deliver the von Eissen piece to the boys at the synagogue Tuesday morning and be done with it. He'd think of what to say to Efrem later, once it was all taken care of. He could tell his son-in-law it was none of his business and say he handled it, even reprimand him for not obeying him in the first place.

He left late in the afternoon once he was somewhat convinced that Efrem was leaving the Burbanks alone for the night. On his way home, Isaac took a detour and scoped out the family's rancher. He could easily make out Nora's room at the front of the house. The window was open and framed with sheer curtains, painted in a warm pink shade, unmistakable for a young lady's bedroom.

Isaac found himself actually grinning as he plotted out what he would do, recalling his boyhood days. More than once on a dare he had broken into stores and neighbor's homes, silently and covertly, not always taking things, other than a trinket or token to prove he'd done it. He was still small and wiry, and he was pleased to realize that even though he was now what he thought of as an old man, he was more agile than people knew. He got a thrill out of having one last adventure. Isaac went home, worked out the details of his plan, including gloves, dark clothing and soft-soled shoes. He waited until late at night to execute his plan.

In his mind, it all worked out so well, but reality spun a different twist. When he first approached the Burbank house around midnight, he saw that Nora's light was on and a young man, who the police later identified as Ralph Johnson, was climbing out of the window. The bedroom light remained on for some time after he left and Isaac returned to his car that was parked down the block and waited. Finally, Nora turned out the light around 1:00 am and he gave her another hour or so to fall into a deep sleep.

Isaac never had any intention of hurting the girl. He just wanted to get in, find the necklace and get out. He had a small penlight that he used for fine work so he thought that would give him enough illumination to search and not disturb her. It took a little more looking than he had figured but he was in too deep to stop and began not to care what he left behind. At last he found the black velvet box tucked away in the dresser. He slipped the necklace into his pocket, but then as he closed the drawer, the noise woke Nora. She sat straight up, her mouth forming an "O" of surprise. Isaac panicked and thought that if he could just give her a little knock, she'd go back down. He grabbed the first thing he saw, gleaming in the ambient streetlight. He swung it with more force than he thought and the royal scepter in his hands packed more punch than he realized. She went down all right, with a sickeningly quiet thud and left a trail of blood that horrified him. He dropped the weapon from his gloved hands and left out the same way he came in with more force than he had intended, cracking the wooden window frame, not sure of what to do next.

All he could do to keep himself sane was to go on with his plans without thinking too much about what had gone terribly, terribly wrong. He checked himself out—his dark clothes were speckled with blood, but not drenched. He could carry on with checking out the two pieces in the shop if he was careful not to leave a trace, then go home and get cleaned up. He was now taking each new step in the night as they came, his plans no longer a reality he could count on. He let himself in at the back of Mendelson's and went immediately to the safe. He almost landed in a dead faint when he opened it and saw that the other piece was no longer there. He relocked the safe, slumped on the floor and began for the first time that night to feel the age in his bones. He guessed that Efrem must have had something to do with it and he didn't know how he was going to handle it. He went home to pray.

In the meantime, Efrem had had his own concerns about the necklace. Oblivious, he had no idea that Isaac had overheard him or that he had any knowledge of anything amiss. He couldn't face Rebecca appearing deceitful regarding her father or his business, so instead of his usual routine of going home to his wife for a pleasant evening, he took a drive and ended up in a bar away from where he thought any of his new found Santa Lucia acquaintances would be. He could sit, think, drink and maybe put his mind at ease, and try to convince himself that it really would be okay to do the exchange in the morning at Poppy Cove, with none the wiser. He began to believe it and relax as he pulled into the parking lot.

He walked into Bud's and sat at the dark, dank bar. To his surprise, there was Dirk Roberts about two drinks in, just beginning to get yappy and jovial. Dirk waved him over and before long, the two were rambling on—the announcer about his ex-wife and winning her over, Efrem referring to a stupid mistake he'd made, regarding the necklace. All the while, Eddie was lurking back and forth from the main saloon to the back lounge with Irene eventually in tow. Dirk kept pestering Efrem about jewelry and how he could win back Kitty with that one special piece. Efrem kept brushing him off, but as the night and the drinks wore on, he found himself thinking more and more about it, and against his better judgment, wanted to fix the problem he believed he had created. He decided he would take his mistakenly placed replica copy out of the Mendelson safe and get the real one that Isaac had created one back, even if he had to do it in the middle of the night and wake up the Burbanks to do so.

It was around midnight when he pulled up to the store and took the velvet case containing the necklace out of the safe. He poured himself back in the car, drunkenly coasting through the streets of Santa Lucia, eventually finding the street name and number of the Burbank household. He saw the dark house and had enough common sense to park around the corner. There he sat and talked out loud to himself, rehearsing in the car what he would say to them. He began to laugh, thinking it was funny and a little crazy, as the alcohol was beginning to wear off. As he sat, sleep began to take over. He shook his head, thinking that he would wait for first morning light before approaching the family. That would still give him plenty of time to straighten everything out before Isaac came in to work. In his warped mind, Efrem even grinned at the thought of how proud his wife would be for taking care of everything, forgetting that he hadn't even called her. He would do that, but first, he'd just take a little nap, right there in the car. He reached into his coat pocket, relieved to feel the gems in his hand and promptly fell asleep. The next thing he knew, he was awakened by the police and taken in for questioning in the robbery and murder of Nora Burbank.

CHAPTER TWENTY-ONE

"I can't believe all this over a necklace!" Daphne exclaimed, as she folded up the day's copy of the *Santa Lucia Times.*

"Is that it? There's got to be more." Margot was propped up in her hospital bed, her ankle starting to hurt just that little bit less and getting itchy. It had been three days since her fall and Santa Lucia's social quake of the Mendelson saga.

Daphne nodded. "It says that Michael Weathers will continue his exposé tomorrow. If he doesn't win some kind of award for this one, I'll be surprised."

Margot agreed. "It's riveting. I'm still so shocked at it all. I have to say that when I realized that Isaac was the one who knocked me down after trying to smother his own son-in-law, I came very close to just disbelieving it. At first I thought it was just a bad dream from the pain and medication, but now..." She shook her head.

Daphne poured her more coffee from the thermal carafe that Lana from the Tearoom had sent over, along with a huge box of Margot's favorite muffins, containing more than the girls could eat. "Poor Rebecca. She's so upset. She loves her father and still can't believe he could do such a thing."

"How's Efrem?"

Daphne chewed her bite of strawberry muffin before replying. "He's doing well. He's pretty much remembered everything that happened up to the point of being knocked out at the track and telling the police all

206 Death of a Beauty Queen

he knows. Thank God he doesn't remember anything about Isaac going after him with the pillow." She gave a little shudder before continuing. "They're sending him home today or tomorrow. He'll have nurses around the clock for a while, but the doctors are confident he'll make a full recovery, just like you."

"I can't wait to get out of here," Margot sighed impatiently.

"Have they said when they'll spring you?"

"No. They keep saying every day, 'in a day or two.' I don't know what that means anymore."

"It means when you no longer need the traction sling for your ankle," a starchy nurse came in and fluffed up her pillows and read her charts. "You'll be fine, but you've had quite the break, Miss Williams. We need to keep the pressure off so the bones knit back strong and healthy. For now, just rest," she remarked as she left.

"Easy for her to say." Margot rolled her eyes and sighed. "What's going on at Poppy Cove? How are the orders coming along? It must be chaotic. I have to get back."

Daphne smiled. It was a bit disorganized. There were many orders coming in from the show, appointments had to be rescheduled, orders filled and/or changed. Marjorie and the rest of the staff were doing their best, but Margot was sorely missed. "We're fine. We miss you, but it's all under control," she replied with an almost convincing stretch of truth. *At least it will be by time you get back,* she thought to herself.

Margot gave her business partner a disbelieving frown, but knew she couldn't do anything about it. She decided to change the subject. "How's the new mother and baby David?"

Daphne gushed. "Oh, he's so cute, and William's so proud! Grace is feeling pretty good. They're going home at the end of the week."

"And what about you?"

"What about me?"

"How are things with Daniel—have you seen him lately?"

"Oh, yes." She gave an impish grin. "I brought him by to see the baby. You too, but you were asleep."

Margot tried to read the smile on Daphne's face as she tucked a golden lock behind her ear while she spoke of her boyfriend. "So he's been around, sharing your family's good fortune?"

"Yes, but you know, it's just, well, it's..." Daphne trailed off.

"Yes, I know he loves you!" She couldn't resist teasing her friend.

Daphne giggled. "And your Romeo, have you seen Tom much?"

Margot nodded. "He's been by every day. He can't stay long, being so busy, but it's nice. The nurses let us have dinner together."

"That's sweet."

"You know, it really is," Margot softened. Being in the hospital was giving her time to think and Tom was often in her thoughts and plans, more so than ever. She had been so independent over the last few years; it surprised her pleasantly to be thinking more and more about her future in terms of 'ours' instead of 'mine.'

Daphne looked around the room, which was filled with bouquets, plants and cards. She read some of the names. "You know, Mar, there's a lot of people who love you in this town. Good Lord, this one's from Nancy Lewis, of all people!" She laughed as she fingered the big, gaudy ostentatious card.

Margot blushed. It had been a long time since she felt at home anywhere and it just was dawning on her now that she did. Maybe she truly could settle down and didn't have to think about what others thought about her and what had brought her to Santa Lucia.

"Well, I have to go," said Daphne. "You know Poppy Cove won't run itself and you need to rest. I'll come by tomorrow with part two!" She waved the *Times* in her hand and left for work. Margot shut her eyes with relief and felt a nap coming on, deeper and more peaceful than she expected.

Friday's issue of the *Times* newspaper was equally as enthralling. Loretta came in with Daphne to recant the reported story, adding more information than the paper would print. Thanks to Lenny Cohen's input, Weathers' headlining crime article focused on what had happened at the track, when Efrem had been knocked out. The story actually started days earlier, picking up from where yesterday's article had ended and related what Isaac had done with the necklace after he discovered Efrem had taken the fake one from the safe.

Isaac had gone home, gotten cleaned up and was too restless to sleep. He took a long drive into the hills, arriving just in time for morning training at the track with a new plan in mind. Lately, he'd been a well-known figure at the races, and giving the excuse of wanting to check out the horses before the next big race on the weekend, he milled about, finding the rental lockers and deciding to hide the necklace in one of them until he knew what to do. He had only guessed that Efrem had taken the piece from the safe but had no knowledge of what his son-in-law had actually done with the necklace the night of his arrest. Or of the fate of Nora—if she was okay, or if the blow had seriously harmed her. He didn't want to think about it and blocked it out of his mind. He drove back down to Santa Lucia and opened up Mendelson's, wondering why Efrem had not shown up, but thought it best to keep quiet, and not to question anything. He decided to just putter away at shop duties and to hopefully avoid the von Eissens and any other trouble that might come his way. When Rebecca called looking for Efrem, he played it cool, acting as if he didn't know anything and was as puzzled as his daughter was about Efrem's being missing. He told Rebecca she shouldn't worry, which was out of character for him, but in her state, she ignored his reaction, called the police and found out what was currently happening to her husband.

Isaac had expected to hear news about the break-in at the Burbank's that morning, and was bereft when the facts came out that Nora had been murdered. He couldn't believe that he could have done such a thing with one blow, but he realized he had. He also knew he had to keep quiet about everything. What he did was unforgivable, but no one must know his terrible secret.

As the stories of the murder of Miss Santa Lucia, the break-in and Efrem's arrest while holding one of the necklaces, surfaced through the day, Isaac considered his options and realized his safest bet would be to play the frail old man. He could be the supportive father to his daughter in such a terrible time, going along with the social set's shock and horror of how this could happen in their town. All the while, he was doing his best to stay in the know with his ear to the ground and avoid Walter and Alex, thinking that he could possibly frame one or both of the von Eissens and turn one of them in for the murder, if necessary. Finding relief in his plan, he actually congratulated himself for his quick thinking in getting his copy of the necklace out of Santa Lucia. As Efrem was a suspect, Mendelson's shop would certainly be searched and he himself could possibly be followed and questioned. He would just give his confused, wide-eyed innocent look to the police. He actually started to believe he could get away with it, hoping that if he made his own private peace with God, his actions might be forgiven before he died.

Walter and Alex von Eissen knew that they were indirectly involved with the murder and robbery through Isaac. They recognized the necklace in the paper and knew they had to either finish off Isaac or their involvement in Santa Lucia, if not both. They called the shop and Isaac's home at all hours during this week, telling him what to do, where to lie low, what not to say and to whom. They told him if he made arrangements for the final exchange, they would spare his and the lives of his loved ones as long as he kept his mouth shut and followed their instructions. At this point, they didn't care what necklace they had, as long as they could fence a good enough piece to their client and move on. When they told Isaac to give them the gems, he told them where the necklace was and they arranged to make the exchange during *The County Cup.* Being that the race was a busy occasion, it would be a good place for it, as so many people would be around that no one would question anyone's presence at such a popular event.

All was working out fine until Isaac was seen by his son-in-law out of the corner his eye at the track that day. Efrem couldn't believe that he saw Isaac there and without saying a word to Rebecca, followed him. He stood at a distance when he saw Isaac go up to a bank of lockers near the stables. He watched with curiosity when he saw the two thugs come up to his father-in-law, who seemed to know them. He couldn't hear what was being said, but he could clearly see that the conversation became heated and thought he should step in. As he called out Isaac's name, the von Eissens spotted him and left, leaving Isaac at the open locker, holding the necklace in his hands.

Efrem was stunned when he realized Isaac was up to no good. He started questioning him to find out what was going on, reached out and snatched the piece roughly, breaking off a section. Isaac panicked and started to leave, running toward the new construction site that was deserted on the Sunday. Efrem caught up with him, grabbed his arm with his free hand and demanded answers. Isaac shook his arm out of the hold and saw the two-by-four saw the two-by-fours piled up for the next day's work and grasped one. He swung, making contact towards the back of Efrem's head. He couldn't believe he did it again and refused to think that he could take another life. He dropped the plank, looked around and saw no one. He put the remaining gems in his pocket. He came across Walter and Alex in a crowd and slipped the partial necklace in Walter's pocket discreetly, saying he was done and if they would say nothing, he would say nothing. The von Eissens nodded and walked away, finding a group to hide in. They might not have been the brightest bulbs in the bunch, but they knew when it was time to fade out.

When the people gathered around Efrem, Isaac waited a few minutes to show up and comfort his poor, distraught Rebecca. He remained loyal and steadfast, ashamed that he might have committed a second murder, but as Efrem's fate was up in the air, no one could say what he would or would not remember. The von Eissen boys made one final contact with Isaac, telling him if he didn't finish off Efrem, they would and take his daughter's life along with his. Isaac's panic continued to override his good sense and seeing that he was in so deep already, he betrayed his daughter's trust again. He stayed close, looking for an opportunity to help Efrem remain asleep forever if he had to. Emotionally he struggled, but felt he was doing the right thing, ultimately protecting his daughter and saving face.

"Okay, I think I know the rest of the story," Margot stated, not wanting to relive her part in that fateful night.

Loretta and Daphne exchanged looks. The reporter folded up the paper and took off her glasses. "Yes, well I'm sure you do."

"What's going to happen to the von Eissens?" Daphne enquired.

"They've been arrested—Walter and Alex, that is. Eddie and Baroness Eva are nowhere to be found."

"Eddie!?!" Margot and Daphne exclaimed at the same time.

"Yes, Eddie. Turns out he's the youngest von Eissen." Loretta wiggled in her chair, straightening up in her self-importance, ready to give her scoop du jour. "He wasn't involved in the gems racket. He was a small time crook, gambling nights and betting, but just penny ante stuff. His big brothers wouldn't let him play with them."

"What about Baroness Eva?" Margot asked.

"She's left town. The boys say she didn't have anything to do with their gem running. They kept Mommy out of it. She might not have even known that the necklace in the show was theirs. From what I've heard, it's just the tip of the iceberg."

"What's going to happen to Isaac?" Margot couldn't help but wonder.

Loretta sighed. "I don't know. It's all so sad, thinking that he could have been a part of this all and obviously guilty of committing murder. They've got him locked away. From what I understand, he's telling the police everything he can and just hoping that Rebecca and Efrem can find it in their hearts to forgive him."

"And what about the Burbanks? I know he says it was an accident, but still he took their daughter's life, all over a bunch of rocks. It's such a tragedy," Daphne added.

The girls sat in silence, contemplating what it all meant. Isaac had been a pillar of the community and driven ultimately by his pride not to accept financial help from loved ones and peers when he needed it. It resulted in unthinkable actions. Coupling these recent events with the not so distant murder of Constance, they wondered if their sleepy little Santa Lucia would ever be the same.

Before long, Loretta broke up the funk with a twinkle in her eye. "Well, there's one thing we do know for sure."

Daphne took the bait, while Margot smiled, knowing exactly what Loretta was going to say. "What's that?"

"Daniel loves Daphne!"

EPILOGUE

By the time Margot was back to work at Poppy Cove, Daphne and the rest of the staff had things under control with just a few minor mix-ups on fabric bolt orders and button selections for Margot to straighten out. However, it took a couple of months hobbling around in a cast and crutches before Margot was back in heels. Irene had certainly helped by pulling extra hours to keep things running smoothly. After her escapade with Eddie, the minor von Eissen hood who hadn't been seen since his older brothers were arrested, she'd been subdued and quiet, staying out of trouble and staying in most nights with her Grandmother.

Isaac had been arrested for the murder of Nora Burbank, robbery and the attempted murder of Efrem. The severity of his punishment was up in the air as he was fully co-operating with the law, which now included the FBI as he was telling them everything he could about the von Eissen's criminal activities. Walter and Alex were mainly involved with money laundering and extortion, but apparently, their little business was just a small part in a bigger crime syndicate that had been going on since the early 1900's. Their father Vladimir was the son of a European crime family head. The European relatives had started by running guns and weapons, along with other black market goods, during World War I. Vladimir had taken the fake name of von Eissen as well as the phony Baron title and had died under mysterious circumstances in New York, where the family had been running bootleg liquor since

Prohibition. The European side of the family leaned heavy on the American von Eissens to move fake gems from their labs after the 'Noble Experiment' and World War II were over. They were cash poor and needed US money to rebuild their empires. They had manufactured well-made impostor gemstones to be sold off as real diamonds. They started in New York and were successful, so they made their way westward by contacting smaller operating branches of the family to coerce desperate jewelers in off-markets to sell in untraceable bigger cities. They had a good thing going for a few years until they hit Isaac, Efrem and Santa Lucia. Baroness Eva von Eissen deserted her sons and is still at large. Her sons claimed she had nothing to do with their transactions.

Efrem Goldberg made a full recovery. He and Rebecca struggled to understand and forgive Isaac for his wrong doings, but it was a long journey. She made sure to visit her father regularly in prison, and Rabbi Hertzfeld met with her often. Mendelson's Jewelers was locked and closed for many weeks. After numerous walks along the beach and endless hours of wave watching, the Goldbergs made the decision together to stay in Santa Lucia and re-open the store as Goldberg Jewelers, creating newer and bolder beautiful collections of necklaces, rings, bracelets and brooches, reflective of Efrem's aesthetics. It took awhile for the Santa Lucians to come around but they eventually did. They could not help but be seduced by the gorgeous new look of the Goldberg variations.

The Miss Santa Lucia crown remained intact, albeit with a few minor shake-ups, which made Mr. Anthony very happy. After too many public temper tantrums, Mary Ann Rutherford was stripped of her position as queen. Caroline Parker stepped in for the rest of the term as Miss Santa Lucia. Fortunately for her and the

Santa Lucians she represented, she stepped in just in time to represent their little town in the Rose Bowl Parade in Pasadena for 1958.

Dr. Edward and Tina Burbank stayed in town, continuing their fine daughter Nora. Isaac had written them a heartfelt letter of apology that remained sealed, waiting for the right time to open it. They drew strength from each other and their community, honoring Nora, and willing to love the memories of her they had.

Daniel did indeed love Daphne and the two were having fun learning about each other on more bowling, dancing, riding and beach dates. Loretta continued chasing her scoops, always looking for the next big story. Margot and Tom grew closer as she recovered from her injuries. He spent more and more time at her house, helping her out with domestic and yard work. He even did some cooking and cleaning, all to the approval of Mr. Cuddles and to the chagrin of Mrs. O'Leary, the neighbor who noticed how his car did not leave the driveway most nights. To Margot's surprise, as she had become accustomed to living alone and enjoying it, having Tom around was quite delightful and she felt lonely when he wasn't there.

One morning over toast, as she was getting ready to put in a full day at Poppy Cove, he looked over at her and said, "Mar, I think we need to talk."

Surprised, she didn't know where he was going. She thought things were fine, but he seemed serious. She gulped her coffee and answered, "Okay."

"I've been here a lot lately," he remarked measured, then paused. She said nothing, waiting for what he might say. "Maybe we should make this a permanent arrangement."

"Oh," she said, putting her coffee cup down on the table. "Do you mean living together?" She'd known of some progressive, artistic couples who lived what was considered 'in sin,' and although she was far from a prude, she wasn't sure she was that liberal either.

"Well, yes. I mean no," he stammered. "Actually, Margot I mean to ask you to marry me."

She blinked, a bit surprised at the question. She really was very happy and in fact comfortable with Tom, more so than she'd been with any man to be honest. But marriage was not on her mind, except to tell others to mind their own business about her affairs. Her mood then darkened. She didn't want to lose him, but she had to risk it. "Tom, there are things you don't know about me."

"And there are things that you don't know about me." He rushed to her side, taking her hand. "Look, I had a life too, before I moved here from San Francisco. All I know is that what I do know about you I like, and I don't think there's anything I could find out that would change that."

"Don't be so sure."

"I'm willing to be."

"What would you say if I needed to think about it?"

"Do you mean about me or about getting married?"

She swallowed hard. "Not you, definitely not you. Marriage."

He stayed strong and smiled. "Don't you want me to make an honest woman out of you, Margot Williams?"

"Give me time, Tom Malone. I live every day trying to be as honest as I can." Her eyes filled with tears.

With all his years of detective training, he still couldn't read if her tears were from happiness, fear, frustration or sadness. He drew her in for an embrace and kissed her passionately, which she returned with equal fire. That was all the answer he needed for now.

THE END

Barbara Jean's Dating Tips for 50's Glamour Girls

- Out on a first date? Order the most expensive item on the menu, whether you like it or not. Watch his reaction—if he smiles, frowns or flinches, that'll tell you if you want to encourage further affections from said man.

- It's okay to be a girl who kisses, but just don't be one who tells. Even the best of the girls did and still do; they just knew how to keep their lips sealed. A grown woman should be allowed to get to know a man who she feels is worthy of her time.

- Know your fragrances and the purpose of wearing them. Youth Dew and Chanel No. 5 are appropriate for the initial *How do you do?* phase. Save Emeraude and Tabu for the intimate *How did you do that?* phase.

- Be a good sport. Surprise dating events add spice to a stale relationship. Fix a fancy meal on a Wednesday, go bowling in a ball gown or pick up the check. He'll be flattered!

- Speaking of flattering, he doesn't always have to be right, but every now and then, let him think he is. Be confident in your own mind that you know the truth of your own brilliance!

- Ready to move on to greener pastures? Take him to a swell party with plenty of people. Get him a drink, get him lost in a crowd, preferably of well girdled and well coiffed women and get into your own swing of things.

- Beware of falsies, fake eyelashes and other accoutrements, especially early on in the relationships. Test drive the padding, glues and heel heights around home and a trusty friend or two. Better for mishaps to happen in the privacy of your own home instead of out in public—a flying bust enhancer or spider-like eyelash trail down your cheek could scare away a potential keeper.

- A little harmless flirting never hurt anyone. Give yourself a sway in your step by winking at a construction worker today. Who knows, it may inspire him to get the building done on time and under budget!

- Always have him be the first to call back after the date. If he takes too long, call him 'by accident' (oops, wrong number, giggle and hang up). This action does not count, as it was in error. If, by the third time, he does not respond, take another dip into the gene pool.

- Still not sure what you want in a man? Play the field! Try dating men with different interests and backgrounds. Doctors, teachers, artists, musicians, accountants—have a little fun with them all. Remember, you can't change them no matter how hard you try, but you can have a ball attempting it all the same.

ABOUT THE AUTHORS

 Barbara Jean Coast is the pen name of authors Andrea Taylor and Heather Shkuratoff, both of whom reside in Kelowna, BC, Canada. Barbara Jean, however, is a resident of Santa Lucia, California (eerily similar to Santa Barbara), where she enjoys long lunches, cocktail parties, fancy dinner dates with attractive and attentive gentlemen. Her interests include Alfred Hitchcock movies, reading Carolyn Keene, music by popular musicians, such Frank Sinatra and Tony Bennett, shopping for new dresses, attending society events and always looking fabulous in kitten heels. DEATH OF A BEAUTY QUEEN is the second Poppy Cove Mystery.

 As an avid mystery reader, Heather Shkuratoff joined lifelong friend Andrea Taylor to create the Poppy Cove Mystery series, written under the pen name of Barbara Jean Coast. Growing up in a family of talented crafters and sewers, Heather developed her own skills to become a dressmaker and designer, which helps to give rich detail and character to their stories. She lives in Kelowna, BC, Canada, but spends much time in California, researching for the novels and doing her best to live like Barbara Jean.

 Andrea Taylor always imagined herself being a supersleuth girl detective and writing adventurous stories, full of mystery and intrigue since she was old enough to hold a pencil. She resides in Kelowna, BC, Canada, where she writes under the pen name of Barbara Jean Coast with her co-author friend, Heather Shkuratoff, and travels often to California to further develop the stories and escapades of the Poppy Cove Mysteries. Andrea has also published freelance articles about fashion, current events, and childcare, and is currently blogging on WordPress about creativity and poetry, as well as researching for her own literary novels.

35602398R10133

Made in the USA
Charleston, SC
15 November 2014